The Secret Life of Amanda K. Woods

The Secret Life of

Amanda K. Woods

ANN CAMERON

SCHOLASTIC INC.

New York Toronto London Auckland Sydney
Mexico City New Delhi Hong Kong

Je remercie Georges Barnouin, professeur d'anglais de Mornas,
France, qui m'a aidé à écrire les "fautes" des lettres d'Antoine.

ISBN 0-439-11551-5

Designed by Caitlin Martin

22 21 20 19 18 17 16   5 6 7 8 9/0

Printed in the U.S.A.   40
First Scholastic printing, September 1999

To my dear friend Susan Ludvigson
finder of four-leaf clovers
who became a poet

and in memory of our teacher
Vivian Anderson

The Secret Life of Amanda K. Woods

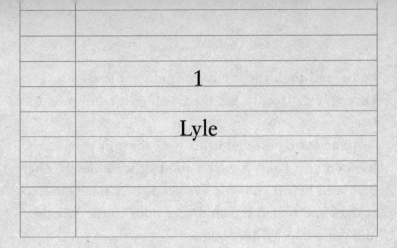

1

Lyle

One summer day Amanda Woods traded her right hand for Lyle Leveridge's. Years later, she would think of that day as the beginning of a new life. At the time, though, she only knew it was the end of something.

It was a Monday in August. Amanda woke late. On the other side of the bed, her sister Margaret's side, the covers were flung back and Margaret was gone. Margaret, who was seventeen, had a summer job at North Wisconsin Hospital. The hospital was in the town of Rome, ten miles away, so Margaret had to wake up early.

Amanda got out of bed and went to the window. Outside, the branches of the oak tree were twisting in the wind. There were big angry waves all across Lost Lake.

Amanda shivered. She dressed, putting on her favorite T-shirt and jeans and her cowboy boots. Then she left the house and took the sandy path along the lake to Lyle Leveridge's place, to get there before it really was too late.

Amanda's family and Lyle's were the only people who lived on Lost Lake. Amanda and Lyle were eleven. They had been best friends for five years, ever since the Leveridges had rented the land next door to the Woodses' and put a house trailer on it.

When Amanda and Lyle were little, they had played with toy cars and trucks, making roads and bridges and towns on a bare earth mound in Lyle's yard. They swam together, and after Amanda got her horse, Skipper, they rode him double, bareback.

Lyle's dad, who worked at the lumberyard in Rome, had built Lyle a shack out of boards so he could have a special place of his own. Little by little, Lyle had filled it with an enormous collection of comic books. On rainy days, he and Amanda read them all day long.

Amanda's mother was an elegant woman who had strong opinions about what was proper. She had made a rule that Amanda couldn't buy comics or have any in her own house. Comics weren't literature, she said. However, she had never said Amanda couldn't read them someplace else. Amanda's mother almost never went over to the Leveridges' place and had never looked into Lyle's shack, so she had no idea how many comics Amanda had read.

Lyle had some Superman, Wonder Woman, Batman, and Captain Marvel comics for light reading. However, his main collection was hundreds of horror comics piled in three stacks on a low wooden table. The stacks reached higher than Amanda's head, and sometimes it seemed to her that there was no end to them.

Lyle told Amanda he read the horror comics to make himself brave. Lyle believed only a very courageous person could read as many horror comics as they had both read.

His collection featured ghosts, ghouls, werewolves, zombies, vampires, and the walking dead. Sometimes Amanda would read Lyle's comics all afternoon, staring at exploding heads or green blood dripping from slashed throats or decaying zombies bursting out of graves, till she felt almost sick and a little scared. Then, as it began to get too dark to read in the shack, Lyle would hand her a Captain Marvel comic to calm down with. When she had to leave to go home for supper, Lyle would say Captain Marvel's magic word, *Shazam!,* giving Amanda the courage to run home, full speed, so she never saw what might be lurking in the shadows.

Pushed by the wind, Amanda climbed up the hill from the lake to Lyle's place, where everything was changed. The Leveridges' lawn chairs were gone, and so was their rusty barbecue grill. Lyle's shack was gone, too. Lyle's dad had taken it down and sold the boards. Now, under the pine tree that had sheltered it, only its hard-packed dirt floor remained. The Leveridges' house trailer had been moved onto the driveway, their aluminum boat upside down on top of it. Lyle and his dad were up on top of the trailer, fastening the ropes to hold the boat.

The Leveridges were moving away, going to Montana. When Lyle had told Amanda they were leaving, she had felt terrible. She'd said, "We'll be friends when we grow up, anyhow." But Lyle had answered, "We'll live far apart and never even know each other."

Amanda realized he was probably right. It seemed as if everybody but her was always right.

She had looked at their hands, which were the same size and exactly the same shade of tan.

"Our hands are the same," she said. "We could change hands. You take one of mine, and I'll take one of yours."

On top of one of the horror comic book stacks, Lyle put his right hand over hers. It covered it exactly.

"We could change hands and no one would know the difference," Lyle said. "But it would be bloody. Too bloody."

Amanda had been disappointed, but glad that at least he hadn't said it was a stupid idea or that he didn't want her hand, anyway.

She ran up to the trailer and Lyle saw her.

"We're almost ready!" Lyle shouted into the wind. He looked excited.

"I got to keep my comics," he added. "My dad fitted them into the boat!"

Lyle's mother came out of the trailer. "What a cold day for leaving," she said. The wind blew her light brown hair, the same color as Lyle's and Amanda's, into her eyes, and she brushed it back.

Lyle's dad helped Lyle down from the roof of the trailer. Lyle's parents both hugged Amanda.

"I hope you like Montana," Amanda said.

"You be good," Mr. Leveridge said. "We'll miss you."

Lyle looked at Amanda and moved his head slightly in the direction of where the shack had been.

Together they walked over there and stood in the middle of the old floor.

"It was nice," Amanda said.

"Yup," Lyle said.

Lyle took her right hand. He pressed the fingers of his right hand against her fingers, the back of his hand against her palm. "Shazam!" he said. He pulled his hand away from hers and shook it three times. Amanda copied him and shook hers three times, too. A funny tingling sensation went up to her elbow.

Lyle was a person who could do almost anything. Amanda thought he might have actually done magic.

The Leveridges' car hiccupped, and then made a stronger sound, more like a tiger's roar. The horn made a tiny beep.

"Lyle, time to roll," Mr. Leveridge called. The trailer was closed up. Lyle's parents were in the car.

"I won't say it!" Lyle told Amanda.

Amanda wanted to ask him what wouldn't he say, but she couldn't, he was already running for the car.

Maybe what he meant was he wouldn't say the word "goodbye."

Amanda didn't say it either.

Lyle jumped in the backseat of the car. He rolled his window all the way down and stuck his head out. His eyes met Amanda's, and he smiled as if they shared some secret about life that nobody else knew, that would be just theirs forever.

The car, with the trailer and boat behind it, bumped slowly down the driveway.

Lyle waved his right hand, or was it Amanda's?

Amanda's right hand—or was it Lyle's?—waved back.

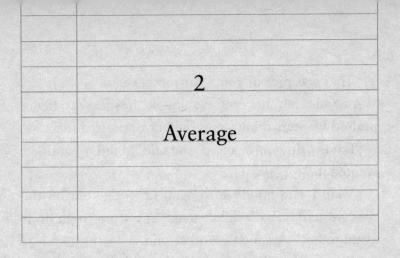

2

Average

Amanda's mother, holding the garden hose, checked the soil in a flower box under the kitchen window, her face deep in pink and white petunias.

"Amanda," she said, "would you turn the water on?"

Amanda opened the faucet—not much, just a little, so the water would soak into the soil slowly.

"That's just right," her mother said.

Amanda felt good. Her mother was very particular, and Amanda hardly ever got anything just right for her.

She and her mother watched the water flow among the petunias.

"At least these are sheltered from the wind," her mother said. "The flowers that face the lake are a mess. Did you say goodbye to the Leveridges?"

"Yes," Amanda said.

"That was nice of you," her mother said.

Amanda felt uncomfortable—as if she was being praised for something she shouldn't be praised for.

"I didn't do it to be nice," she said. "I did it because I wanted to."

"Well, I said goodbye to Mrs. Leveridge out on the road yesterday, so it didn't make any sense to go do it again today," Amanda's mother said.

"I'm sure you'll miss Lyle," she added, "but it's for the best."

Amanda hunched her shoulders. Her new right hand, which had been vibrating with unknown powers, began to go numb.

Why was it that when her mother wanted her to feel better, she so often made Amanda feel worse? Especially when she said something was "for the best."

But Amanda knew what her mother meant. Her mother had often said that Lost Lake needed "a better class of people." She always hoped that the best families from Rome would buy land and build homes on Lost Lake.

Where pine trees massed against the far shore, her mother could imagine the lights of a little village forming—a village of people like the Woodses who would build nice houses and plant petunias and appreciate beauty. Not people like the Leveridges, who lived in trailers and built shacks.

When Amanda thought of how her mother felt about the Leveridges, it made her feel very sad. Her mother saw the sadness in her face.

"Straighten your shoulders and don't mope, Amanda!" her mother said. "Moping is so unattractive."

Amanda didn't want to be unattractive. Sometimes she was afraid she was. She opened her eyes wide and lifted the corners of her lips in her "I am not moping" expression. Woodses were successful people who didn't mope. If you wanted to be a Woods, you had better not do it.

"That's better," her mother said. She studied Amanda for a moment.

"You need to keep yourself occupied," she said. "Make us some blueberry muffins."

Amanda turned the water off, coiled the hose, and followed her mother into the house. Her mother paused at the door of her office. Papers were heaped up on the desk inside; her mother was in the middle of paying bills. Amanda's father owned the Rome Hotel and managed it himself. Her mother helped by keeping all the hotel's accounts.

"I've an awful lot to catch up on right now," she said. "Do you think you can make the muffins by yourself?"

"I guess so," Amanda said.

She went into the kitchen. The clouds outside made its

white cupboards and white walls look gray. She started the steps of making muffins, but it was hard. The weather, she thought, was sticking everything together. The cookbook didn't want to open, the oven didn't want to light, the oil and eggs didn't want to be beaten, the milk and then the flour didn't want to mix in.

Amanda set her spoon down. Where was Lyle, she wondered. A long way down the road for sure. Maybe this far from him his hand wasn't even any good.

But she made a fist to get the feeling of power back into it, and that worked. Then she pretended she was her hero, the Lone Ranger, the handsome masked man on TV, who galloped across the Wild West, bringing happiness and justice wherever he went. The Lone Ranger, who, in order to bring peace to the world and defeat evil, had to make blueberry muffins. For something so important, it could be done.

Sunlight flew in the window, the blueberries tumbled into the batter, the batter swam into the muffin tin, and the tin slid into the oven without a drop spilled.

It was only when the muffins were baking that Amanda remembered she hadn't greased the tin.

Amanda stuck her head in the door of her mother's office.

Her mother, punching numbers on her adding machine, looked up.

"I forgot to grease the tin," Amanda said, "so what should I do?"

"Good heavenly gracious!" her mother said. "There's nothing you can do! How could you forget, Amanda?"

"I don't know, I just did," Amanda said.

"You need to pay attention to what you're doing," her mother said. "You can't be always dreaming."

"I'm not always dreaming!" Amanda protested.

Her mother pressed the ADD button on the gray steel machine, which with whirring and grinding sounds printed out a total. It seemed to be calculating the exact sum of Amanda.

"You are," her mother said, "practically always dreaming."

"I'm not!" Amanda said.

Amanda knew she wasn't always dreaming. When she was little, it was true, she had spent a lot of time pulling on her elbow, but nobody could call that dreaming. She had done it for a reason.

Her father had told her that if she could kiss her elbow, she could actually turn into a boy, so of course she tried, but no matter how she hauled on her elbow it never got close enough to her mouth for the kiss, and she remained a girl.

She still did spend some time in her head pretending to be the Lone Ranger, or at least a boy, but pretending was not dreaming.

"The muffins look okay," Amanda added, trying to sound practical. "I checked and they're rising. They smell wonderful."

"Yes, but when you take them out of the tin they are going to stick and come out crumbs."

"They could still be good to eat anyway," Amanda said stubbornly.

"Yes, if you don't care how things look. If you think we'd really want to have a plate of crumbs with dinner."

Amanda tried to think of an attractive way to serve crumbs. Maybe with milk and more blueberries on top. But there weren't any more blueberries. Just crumbs and milk?

"You need to care about appearances, Amanda. Appearances are—well, I wouldn't say they are what matters most in life, but they are very important. How food looks is almost as important as how it tastes. The best thing you can do with those muffins is give them to Skipper."

Amanda took the muffins from the oven and set the tin on top of the stove to cool. They still smelled wonderful. They looked beautiful. If she just put them on the table in the tin, everybody would see how good they looked, and they could remember that while they ate the crumbs. If appearances weren't good, couldn't people just close their eyes and taste? If appearances were so so SO important, God would not have given people eyelids.

Amanda thought of telling her mother this. Instead, she took a knife and, with her lucky Lyle Leveridge right hand, carefully loosened one muffin from the tin. It didn't come out crumbs! It came out in eleven pieces. There were very few actual crumbs. The trouble was, what to other people was a piece of something, to Amanda's mother was a crumb.

Amanda gently picked up the muffin pieces and set them on a plate. By the time she had them on the plate, there were fourteen not-so-large muffin pieces. Amanda ate one. It was good.

Lyle, she was sure, would have liked the muffin. Lyle would have eaten it and said it was delicious. Maybe even his parents would have eaten it. On the other hand, maybe not. Probably not.

Amanda suddenly felt as if she were getting a cold, or a fever, or some deadly disease. This was how she usually felt when she had failed her mother. The only thing was, she probably wouldn't get sick. She was too healthy, that was the trouble.

If she actually did get sick, she knew her mother would be very concerned about her, and bring her meals in bed, and touch Amanda's forehead with a cool hand. This had happened a few times.

Amanda hung on to the kitchen cabinets, thinking she might be dizzy, wishing the fever would really come, so her mother would have a reason to forget her faults.

She wished she could sink down on the floor gracefully, a fainting victim. However, her Lyle Leveridge right hand wouldn't let go of the cabinet; neither would her not so special but practical left hand. Hitting the floor would hurt, that was why.

Amanda sighed. She took the knife and picked all the muffins out of the tin. There were quite a few pieces—so many she didn't want to count them. She put them on the plate and then carried them outside, whistling for Skipper.

By the time she got to the pasture fence, Skipper was already there, pressing his chest against it, his caramel-brown head held high and his ears pricked up. Skipper liked treats.

She put muffin pieces in the palm of her Lyle Leveridge hand and held them under Skipper's velvety nose. With two sweeps of his soft lips across Amanda's palm, he got them all. Then he reached out to the plate in her left hand and finished the rest.

"They were really good, weren't they?" Amanda said. Skipper nodded, arching the whole length of his beautiful neck.

She rubbed the white star on his forehead and hugged

him. People are too picky, Amanda thought. She wondered how life would be if she had been born a horse. Better, probably.

When she went back inside, she could hear her mother on the phone. She started cleaning up the kitchen, half listening to her mother's phone voice, smooth and confident, like a river that always knew where it was going.

Amanda heard Margaret's name. Putting the muffin tin away, she went to eavesdrop, standing outside the office door.

"Seventeen. She's outstanding," her mother was saying proudly. "She'll be applying to some very good colleges this fall." There was a pause, then her mother added, "Amanda is my other daughter . . . Eleven . . . She's average, but she's very sweet."

Amanda didn't want to hear any more. She walked rapidly down the hall to the room she shared with Margaret. She stared at her bookshelf, which was almost empty, and at Margaret's, which was crammed full, and at the bulletin board full of newspaper clippings about Margaret's successes. There were photos of Margaret with class officers, being junior class vice president (the highest office a girl could win, since everybody knew a boy had to be president); Margaret at the state debate tournament, with a trophy in her arms; Margaret wearing her nurse's aide uniform and a surgical mask, working at North Wisconsin Hospital; Margaret in the junior prom court in a long dress; and many, many more.

Amanda passed Margaret's fancy dressing table with the mirror above it, trying not to look at herself. She threw herself down on her and Margaret's bed and clutched her lucky new right hand with her old left hand. Her new right hand felt dead.

Amanda's head throbbed with something sort of like a headache but not exactly, and she rubbed it into her pillow as deep as it would go. Then she cried because she couldn't help being average, and she had lost her best friend in the world.

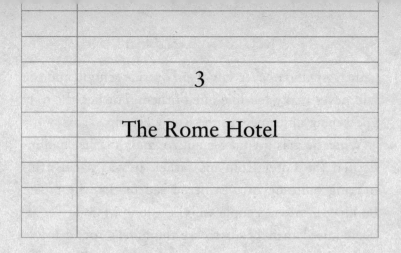

3

The Rome Hotel

Amanda was delving into her and Margaret's closet, pulling out wrinkled blouses that needed ironing and skirts that would have to be lengthened by her mother. It was too bad, because Lincoln School in Rome, where Amanda would once again be going, was not worth the trouble.

Amanda had always wanted to go to school out in the country, at the one-room schoolhouse near Lost Lake where the farm kids went, but she never could. Like Lyle's parents, her parents had always made her go to school in Rome: they thought that in a bigger school, with a different teacher for each grade, she would get a better education.

The other kids who went to Lincoln School in Rome had all grown up in the same neighborhoods playing together. Amanda never saw them outside school, and she had never really felt like one of them. For her, the only good thing in Rome was the Rome Hotel.

When he was a young man, Amanda's father had inherited the hotel from his father. It was a cheerful-looking building of weathered red bricks, the tallest building in town. People walking along Main Street always raised their heads to see the hotel's round tower with a belt of stars in stucco under the window and a weather vane on the top. Amanda figured that everybody was probably proud that Rome had a building so tall.

The hotel was like a second home to Amanda. From when she was little she had known the clerks at the registration desk, the cleaning ladies and the waitresses, the bartenders, and Charley, the cook. She liked them all, but Charley was her favorite. Now that she was older, she did her homework at the hotel every afternoon, waiting for her dad to finish work and drive back to Lost Lake.

The Rome Hotel was the only hotel in Rome, and it had been popular with travelers for a long time. However, it had become a worry to her dad. When three motels were built on the edge of town, cutting into his business, her dad had gotten a big bank loan and spent a lot of money remodeling. Now the hotel was attracting many travelers again. Because it wasn't just nice, it was unique.

Besides having new carpeting and wallpaper and lights, it had become almost a museum for the history of Rome. In the halls, the dining room, and the lobby her dad had hung historic pictures of Wisconsin: portraits of the Indians who had once roamed all its forests but who hardly left their reservations now; photographs of the loggers who cut down the forests, standing proudly by enormous logs; pictures of sledges loaded with logs being pulled by teams of oxen with steaming breath; and portraits of the farm families that settled around Rome after all the timber was gone.

The dining room of the Rome Hotel was called the Loggers' Inn. On its walls hung kerosene lamps like those used in the old logging camps, and logging tools rested on low shelves beside descriptions of how they had been used. There was a long two-man saw with handles on both ends, huge tongs that had clamped on logs so horses could pull them, cant hooks for rolling logs, and snowball hammers for knocking the snow out from under horses' hooves.

Near the hotel's reception desk, a branding hammer with the letters "KS" on its head sat on top of a huge slice of an old log. The same letters were driven deep into the end of the log. Amanda's father had explained to her how in the spring, when the ice on the river melted, loggers had moved thousands and thousands of logs belonging to different companies downriver. The brands hammered into the ends of the logs had made it possible to see whose logs were whose.

In the bar next to the restaurant hung a big horn called a gabreel. It had been used in a logging camp to call the men to dinner. Nowadays, when somebody blew it in the Rome Hotel bar, it meant he would buy drinks for everybody. An old player piano her father had found at an auction was in there, too. Rolls of paper with holes in them made the player piano's keys strike as if they were being hammered by a ghost. The piano played old songs you never heard on the radio. It cost only ten cents to play it, and in the summer, when vacationers came through Rome, they had it going all the time.

To Amanda, being in the hotel after it had been remodeled was like breathing the air of another time. But it might have been completely different, because at first Amanda's mother and dad had disagreed about how to redesign it.

Amanda's mother said the dining room would look like a barn with all those tools in it. Her father said nobody knew what a barn looked like anymore, so that was probably a good thing.

Amanda's mother said she thought the hotel would do

better if the whole building was done over in the style of the great Wisconsin architect Frank Lloyd Wright, who was a genius.

Her dad agreed that Frank Lloyd Wright was a genius, but he said that if they were to redo the Rome Hotel in his style, they would have to tear down the whole building and begin again from the ground up. Besides, he said, nobody ever got anywhere by copying a genius.

What had surprised Amanda most about that argument was first, that her father had argued at all, and second, that her mother had lost.

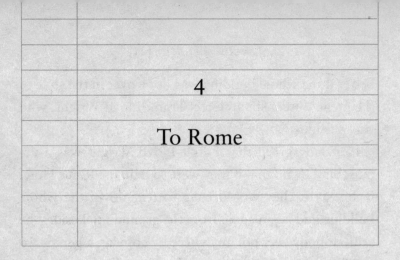

4

To Rome

The family station wagon bumped down the dirt road from Lost Lake to the highway. Amanda sat gingerly on the leather seat, looking down at her well-shined oxfords, missing her cowboy boots. She sat straight, trying to avoid wrinkling her white blouse and her red plaid skirt. She felt like a carefully wrapped present that somebody had to deliver in perfect condition.

The somebody, of course, was her father, who was wearing a business suit, a blue-and-white tie, a homburg hat, and a frown.

Trees, then farms with big white farmhouses, slid by the car window. At the side of the road, farm kids carried metal lunch boxes and walked together toward their one-room country school. Amanda waved at a boy and girl. She didn't know them, but they still waved back.

Someday Amanda would be like Margaret and ride the school bus into Rome for high school with the other country kids. Then she would get to know them. But that was a long time off.

Lyle had gone to Franklin School in Rome, near the lumberyard where his dad worked. In the old days, they had ridden into town together.

She wondered about Lyle starting school in Montana. It couldn't be any worse than Lincoln School, where she had no friends.

Amanda looked at her dad. He had taught her everything in life that really counted: how to ride a horse, how to shoot a gun, how to fish, how to swim and dive and water-ski. But he was hard to talk to.

"When you were a kid, did you have a lot of friends?" Amanda asked.

"No," he said.

Amanda couldn't believe it. Everybody must have loved him always. She had looked into his high-school yearbook once, where a girl named Emily had written: "George, you are the best dancer!" Everybody, not just Emily, must have liked him! She was almost angry at him that he said it wasn't true.

"Why didn't you have friends?"

"We lived in the country, maybe that was why. It's a long time back, Amanda. I really don't remember much." He sounded bored and impatient.

How could a person forget his own life, Amanda thought, but she said nothing.

They passed the Red Cedar Cheese Factory, with its shiny aluminum roof. It marked the halfway point to Rome. Her dad looked at his watch and speeded up.

The night before, Amanda and her dad had taken their boat out on Lost Lake to fish. She had felt very close to him.

A new moon had appeared like a second boat, bright yellow, floating in the darkening sky. On the lake, the tangled smells of dark and water, of green and damp, had tugged at them.

Birds had rustled in the willows, settling down to sleep, and farther off, out of sight, as if it was searching everywhere for someone, an owl demanded harshly, "Who? Who? Who?"

"If I knew, I would tell you," Amanda had thought.

Amanda had caught two northern pike, bringing them in just right.

Her dad had been proud of her. He didn't think the way Amanda's mother did, that Amanda always got things wrong.

She had thought of a line from a book: "We are of one blood, he and I." Being of one blood meant more than being father and daughter, or mother and daughter, or sisters. It meant being the same kind of people.

She and her dad, she thought, were the same kind of people.

But now Amanda felt as if Lost Lake had evaporated and there was not a drop of it left, or a drop of the closeness with her father. She looked at his face. From the side, it looked like the face on a coin, handsome, but hard and unmoving.

They got to the sign that marked the entry to Rome— "Rome, Wisconsin, pop. 6,594"—and her dad slowed up but looked at his watch again. "I don't want you late on the first day of school," he said.

Amanda didn't answer. He would be angry if she said she would just as soon be late, on the first day and the second day and every day. And she didn't have anything else to say. Besides, she knew her dad didn't want to talk. Same blood or not, that was the way he was.

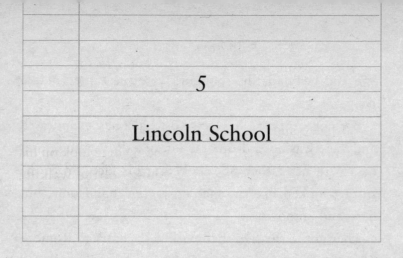

5

Lincoln School

Amanda ran down the empty main hall at Lincoln School, where you were never supposed to run. At the corner where the stairs began, she almost ran into the principal. Miss Deverest was wearing one of her many brown dresses, the exact color of the dull bricks of Lincoln School.

"Amanda, no running!" she said. She had been Amanda's third-grade teacher. Amanda thought she had a special glint of dislike in her eyes, but who could tell? Even Margaret said the Lincoln School teachers hadn't been standing in line when God passed out the smiles.

You could only guess how they actually felt about anything. It seemed as if they didn't hate children, but they didn't like them, either. They didn't hate teaching, but probably they didn't especially like it, either. It seemed as if they weren't happy, but they weren't happy, either.

When Amanda had described them to Lyle, he had got a bright-eyed, feverish horror-comic-reading look on his face and said, "Lincoln School, home of the walking dead!"

Amanda, not exactly running, hurried to the top of the stairs. The new fifth graders were crowding into their new room. Amanda's place, as usual, was in the back corner of the room, next to the windows. She always got that place because her name began with "W," and she was glad, because it meant she could watch the family of squirrels that lived in the maple tree out the window. Also, she could read library books under her regular books, unnoticed, and pretend she wasn't at Lincoln School.

Mary Jane Stoltenberg, as usual, sat next to her. Amanda didn't like Mary Jane from way back, from second grade, when Mary Jane had talked about nothing but her precious paper doll collection and the fourteen sets of outfits she had for each doll, and every girl but Amanda had thought it was *so* interesting. At that time Amanda had frankly told Mary Jane and everybody else that paper dolls were for sissies.

Now Mary Jane's gaze skidded across Amanda's face, but while Amanda was actually thinking of saying a friendly hello, Mary Jane looked elsewhere.

Kids talked to one another and opened desks to see if any old bubble gum was still stuck inside them.

Their new teacher, Miss Vivian Harmon, clapped her hands and said, "People!"

There was silence. Amanda looked around for the people, a word that in her experience always meant grownups.

"People," said Miss Harmon, "may I have your attention?" and then Amanda realized Miss Harmon was calling *them* people.

It was nice to be called people, Amanda thought. Because if the fifth grade was people, then each one of them was part of a people—a person. A person, not just a child.

Miss Harmon had thick, very blond hair like the singer Patti Page, and she wore a blue dress with a design of red balloons on it. She told the class she was from Los Angeles, California. She'd come to Rome for the clear air, she said, because the smog in Los Angeles was ruining her health. She said being in Rome was an adventure for her, and that she hoped fifth grade would be an adventure for them all. Learning was an adventure, she said, and the more people learned, the more interesting lives they could have.

Then Miss Harmon gave them a writing assignment— not "What I Did on My Summer Vacation," which everyone expected, but "What I Like to Do Best, and How I Do It."

Amanda wrote about riding Skipper. "He is not just a horse, he is my friend," she wrote. When everybody had finished writing, Miss Harmon had them all take turns reading their papers out loud to the whole class.

Amanda figured Mary Jane Stoltenberg would read about her dumb paper dolls and their fourteen sets of clothes and how she worshipped them and salivated over them and cried when they fell apart. But Mary Jane didn't: she read about taking a trip to the Atlantic Ocean and learning how to sail and collecting shells, and how big the ocean looked, so big it made you feel you could see to the end of the world.

Amanda thought Pamela Collins would read a paper about liking school, because she was always a teacher's pet; but she didn't, she read about how much she liked to sing.

Nobody was the way Amanda thought they were, especially the girls.

At recess, while the boys played kickball, the girls gathered in the grassy place by the chain fence that roped off the school's front lawn from the playground. For years Amanda had played with boys, but in fourth grade boys had stopped playing with girls. In fourth grade Amanda had mostly stood around, thinking about when she could get back to Lost Lake to play with Lyle. But now Lyle was gone.

The personal things the girls had read about themselves made Amanda want to be friends. Slowly, as if she didn't have a direction really, she edged up to them, but they didn't notice her and nobody greeted her. They all went on talking to one another about things they had done together over the summer in Rome. Amanda stood behind Mary Jane Stoltenberg's shoulder, listening. Then Mary Jane Stoltenberg stepped backward, landing hard on Amanda's foot. It must have been an accident Mary Jane didn't realize happened, because she didn't even say "Excuse me." Still, Amanda couldn't help thinking maybe it wasn't an accident.

She walked away stiffly, imitating the walk the Lone Ranger used on TV. She didn't want to go near the boys playing kickball, so she bent down and pretended to study the sunken asphalt in the middle of the playground with a keen-eyed Lone Ranger look. But she didn't feel like the Lone Ranger. She felt like a rock that had fallen from the sky.

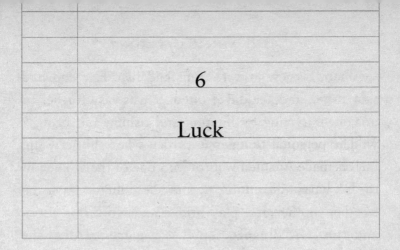

6

Luck

Even on a Saturday morning, her father was at work. Margaret and her mother were down on the beach, slathered with suntan lotion, trying to keep their tans.

Amanda sat in the living room looking at cartoons in the *Saturday Evening Post*. They were mostly about foolish women—women who were bad drivers, who couldn't decide what they wanted, or who spent lots of money buying things that they thought made them look good but that were really ugly.

The cartoons were funny, but when Amanda hit one about a woman who always burned dinner, somehow it reminded her of the blueberry muffins and she closed the magazine. She started leafing through her dad's *Outdoor Life,* with paintings of brave and daring men up in Alaska hunting gigantic grizzly bears and reeling in huge fish.

Amanda knew how to hunt and fish. Her dad had taught her, and she did it often. It was easy for her to imagine surviving by hunting and fishing and being a wilderness guide or a game warden when she grew up, but she never wanted to turn into one of the women in the *Saturday Evening Post*, and she didn't want to be like her mother and play bridge and work in politics and run civic organizations. As a game warden, she could capture hunters who shot animals out of season and take them off to jail. Skipper would help her. Of course, by the time she was a game warden, he would be very old. She closed the magazine and went outside to see him.

He was standing at the fence, as if he'd been waiting for her.

"Do you want to go for a ride, boy?" Amanda asked, and Skipper nodded.

She got his saddle and bridle from the tack room next to his stall. Skipper dipped his head and opened his mouth so she could slip the bit of the bridle into it, and she rubbed him behind the ears to thank him.

Amanda saddled Skipper and lifted herself into the saddle, and Skipper took off.

He galloped a long way down the dirt road; then, where a shadowy old logging trail almost intersected it, Amanda raised his reins to slow him down.

"Whoa, boy," she said.

She wanted to ride the old logging trail, a road she had never traveled. To herself, Amanda always called it the ghost road. It curved off north, just a narrow break in the trees, with ferns and grass instead of pavement. Seventy years before, her father said, oxen had hauled logs out of the forest over an icy track as lumbermen urged them on. Though the road had never been used since, the weight of the sledges they pulled had compressed the earth so no trees could grow in it. In another hundred years, her father said, it would still be there, a trace of a far-gone past.

They turned onto the old trail, a tunnel of shadowy green with birds skimming through it. Skipper picked his way along it delicately, avoiding fallen branches. Amanda wondered how far it would go—maybe to Canada, she thought. If it did, she wished someday she would have the courage to follow it that far north to land so wild it had no boundaries. Sometimes when she left home on Skipper, she never wanted to go back.

She was just beginning to worry about how far they really might be going when she saw brightness ahead, and suddenly the narrow road opened into a meadow.

It was blazing with sun and wildflowers: black-eyed susans, with deep yellow petals and chocolate-brown centers, and goldenrod starting to turn from gold to white. A crow wheeled above it in black circles, cawing hoarsely, its voice like ice in the September sky.

The sound sent a shiver of loneliness through Amanda, but still she loved the beauty of the meadow, the privilege of seeing it. She watched as the crow flew north; then she dismounted and loosened Skipper's reins so he could lower his head to graze. The meadow was the most beautiful place Amanda had ever seen.

She sat down on a fallen log, wishing Lyle were with her. What would he have said about her being average, she wondered. Maybe he would have said, "Average people can be smart. Average people can be lucky."

She said it out loud to herself, the way she thought Lyle might have said it. It sounded true. And then, almost like a sign that it was true, in the grass she saw a four-leaf clover.

Everybody said four-leaf clovers were lucky. In the summer, kids spent hours and hours trying to find them. Amanda had never found one before. She picked it with her right hand, her Lyle Leveridge hand, and put it in the pocket of her shirt.

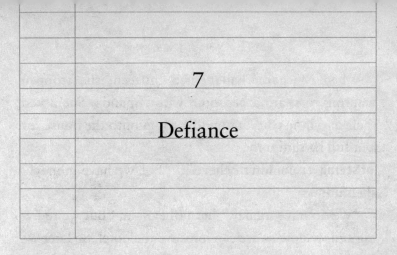

7

Defiance

Amanda knew that putting up her clover in her and Margaret's room might cause a fight with Margaret, but she did it anyway.

She rolled a little bit of melted candle wax into a soft white circle. Then she stuck the circle in the exact middle of the headboard of her and Margaret's bed—at the top, where neither of them would bump it. Holding the four-leaf clover gently, she pressed it into the wax.

Then she waited for it to fall down, but it didn't—she was a success. It stayed right where she put it, radiating peace and luck. Amanda sat on the bed, waiting for Margaret to show up.

Amanda and Margaret were sisters, but they didn't get along. In a roundabout way, the Rome Hotel was the reason.

When Margaret had turned thirteen, she stopped wanting to share a bedroom with Amanda. She asked their dad if he couldn't build a room onto the house for her, but he said no.

Margaret couldn't believe it. "But we have money!" she said.

"We do have money," her father said, "But we're living simply now so we can improve the hotel. So later we can live better. Later I'm almost sure you can have your own room."

Margaret, looking as if she would cry, had said, "Can't I at least have my own bed?" But it turned out that two beds wouldn't fit into the room with all the other stuff they had. Their dad had said he was sorry, but "suffering is good for the soul." That was one of his favorite sayings, but Amanda didn't know if he really meant it.

Anyhow, Amanda didn't think Margaret suffered so much from not having a room of her own. A lot of Margaret's own friends shared rooms and beds with little sisters. But from that time on, Margaret had made Amanda suffer, because when Margaret didn't get her way, she turned into the boss of the room.

She treated Amanda like a mosquito. Like a mosquito in her room that, just because it was a mosquito, couldn't do anything right.

If Amanda opened the window, Margaret made her

close it. If Amanda whistled, Margaret said it sounded horrible and made her stop. If Amanda left something lying around, Margaret made her pick it up. If Amanda wanted two blankets, Margaret wanted only one. Besides that, Margaret complained that in the night Amanda rolled over onto her side of the bed and collided with her.

Amanda, looking at the four-leaf clover, no longer felt strong vibrations of peace. She began to feel nervous. She stood up, shaking her Lyle Leveridge hand, then held it up high, palm facing west, toward Montana.

"What should I do if she makes me take it down?" she asked Lyle.

It took a long time before a Lyle thought came.

It was "Why can she make you?"

"She always does," Amanda said.

Another Lyle thought came then right away. It was "Stand up for your rights."

Margaret walked in, looking hot and sunburnt. She threw her beach towel down on the bed and glanced at its mahogany headboard.

"What is that thing?" she said.

"Anybody can see what it is!" Amanda said.

"Some green bug or something," Margaret said.

"It's not, it's a four-leaf clover!" Amanda said. "I found it."

"Whatever it is," Margaret said, "I don't want it there."

"It's to divide the bed," Amanda said. "You always say I roll over on your side. Now it'll mark the sides. Maybe I won't roll over so much."

"I still don't like it," Margaret said.

"You always think you're the boss!" Amanda said.

"I am not boss of the room," Margaret said. "I am older, that's all, and when something looks stupid, I know it."

"It doesn't look stupid to me," Amanda said. "You have everything else in this room your way! You have a desk. I don't! You have a dresser. I don't! You have the bulletin board."

"That's *our* bulletin board. It's not my fault nothing of yours is on it," Margaret said.

"If I had something to put on it, there wouldn't be any room anyhow," Amanda said.

"Your ego is acting up," Margaret said.

"It is not!" Amanda said.

"Don't be silly," Margaret said. She began to reach toward the clover.

With her Lyle Leveridge hand, Amanda held Margaret's arm away from it.

"Margaret," Amanda cried, "I am a *person*! You are not the only person in this room!"

Margaret paused. "All right," she said, "leave the clover. Until it falls down." She made a face at it and left the room.

"It's going to bring good luck! It's not going to fall down!" Amanda called after her.

She didn't know if that was true. Also Amanda wondered if an ego was something bad. If she had one, did Margaret have one, too? Still, looking at the clover made her very happy. Because she had stood up for it. Because she, just like every other person, had a right to her own ideas, a right to something of her own.

8

In a Cold Climate

"People," Miss Harmon was saying, "people, today we are going to talk about climate, and how it has changed our lives."

In two weeks of school, this was not the most interesting thing Miss Harmon had ever said.

Under Amanda's geography book, a smaller book, *The First Rider,* stuck out. *The First Rider* was an adventure novel Amanda had borrowed from the library. It was very exciting.

The first rider lived in the Caucasus, six thousand years ago. His name was Zorak. He and his tribe grew up among mountains, near a herd of wild horses.

Zorak was the man who first had the idea of riding horses. He tried to persuade his people that they could all do it, but they thought he was crazy for thinking anyone could ever get on top of a horse and stay there, so Zorak decided he was going to have to capture a horse alone.

He took a store of food and a leather water bag, his bow and arrows and a rope, and left his people's camp. Near a river he found the wild horses' tracks and followed them for many days. Sometimes he got close to the horses, but always they caught his scent and ran.

Rocky paths cut Zorak's leather shoes. He ate so little that sometimes he was dizzy. When he was climbing a cliff, a thorn pierced his leather water bag, and all the water ran out. Zorak stopped by a waterfall to patch and refill it. Then he kept on, following the horses until they entered a narrow box canyon.

With a stone ax, Zorak cut down trees to block the entrance to the canyon. Once he was sure that the blockade of trees and branches would trap the horses inside, he climbed over it to get closer to the horses. Inside the canyon, on top of a high rock, the biggest and most beautiful of the wild horses, the one Zorak had seen from a distance and named Red, stared at him and neighed a challenge . . .

"You see, people," Miss Harmon said, "if the weather gets much colder or much hotter, much wetter or much drier, that eventually changes the plants farmers can grow. In the past, whole civilizations died out because the climate changed and they couldn't grow enough food."

Amanda hoped Miss Harmon was concluding.

"One way we track the climate," Miss Harmon said, "is to record temperatures day by day and then calculate the monthly averages. Let's do that now for the month of November last year, right here in Rome," she said—and to Amanda's dismay she quickly wrote thirty numbers on the blackboard.

"Now, people," she said, "would each of you calculate the average temperature in November for me?"

This was not fair, Amanda thought. There was more than enough arithmetic right in arithmetic class. No other teacher made arithmetic show up in the middle of geography. However, she copied the numbers and added them. She did not take time to divide them by 30.

Zorak took his lasso in his wounded and bleeding hands. He called out, "O beautiful red horse, you are mine at last!"

Miss Harmon called out, "Amanda, tell us the average temperature in Rome for November last year."

"It was cold," Amanda said.

Miss Harmon seemed to be waiting for details.

"Very cold," Amanda said. "Cold as the Caucasus."

"Please answer in degrees," Miss Harmon said. Her eyes didn't look friendly.

Amanda rushed to finish the problem. It was hard, because other students were waving their hands. Out of the corner of her eye, she could see Bob Larson making strange motions as if he were writing on his desk top, and Mary Jane Stoltenberg sliding a paper around on her desk. Amanda did her best to ignore them.

The total of all the temperatures was 901. To divide 901 by 30 and get the average, first you could divide it by 10 and then by 3. That would make it easier. Divide it by 10 . . .

Mary Jane Stoltenberg had one hand up, and with the other she was flapping her piece of paper over the side of the desk. *Everybody's* hands were waving. Maybe, since Amanda hadn't answered, Miss Harmon would call on somebody else.

"Amanda!" Miss Harmon demanded.

"Ninety point one degrees," Amanda said. She could feel Miss Harmon's mood, the mood maybe of a teacher waiting for something more.

"Fahrenheit," Amanda added.

Everybody laughed. Miss Harmon frowned.

"People!" she protested, and then she called on Pamela Collins, who had 30.03 degrees, the right answer, just the way Pamela Collins always did.

"How did you get that answer, Pamela?" Miss Harmon asked. And Pamela explained.

At recess, Amanda wasn't feeling good. She wanted to be by herself. She stood like the Lone Ranger, but even that didn't feel too good. She checked her Lyle Leveridge hand. It maybe had power in it, but it seemed detached from the rest of her. She stood by the side of the school where the water fountain was, and used her Lyle Leveridge hand to turn it on and off, as if it had some problem she was studying.

Even though she was busy, Mary Jane Stoltenberg walked straight up to her. Remembering the time Mary Jane had stepped on her, Amanda looked down at her feet to be ready.

But Mary Jane didn't step on her oxfords. Mary Jane said, "I wanted to help you. I stuck that paper with the answer on it practically in front of your face! And Bob was drawing the answer with his fingers."

"You did? He was?" Amanda said. She heard the words, but her mind could not grasp them.

"You don't see anything, do you?" Mary Jane Stoltenberg said.

And then she walked away.

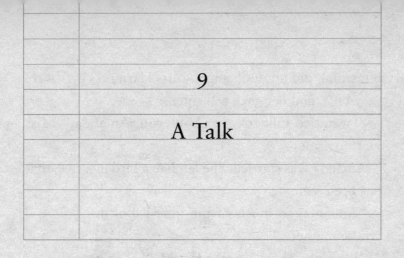

9

A Talk

Miss Harmon arranged some papers on her desk, while Amanda stood beside it, waiting.

She had never ever had to stay after school to see a teacher before. She felt ashamed. She just hoped her parents never found out.

Maybe it was true what Mary Jane said, that at school she usually didn't see things. Now she didn't even want to look at Miss Harmon, so she looked at the empty chairs in the room. All her classmates seemed to be sitting in them, invisible, ready to listen and judge her. There was nothing safe to look at but the floor.

Miss Harmon closed the door to the hallway and pulled up a chair for Amanda next to her desk. Amanda put her books on the floor and sat down.

She looked at Miss Harmon's face. It was not smiling,

but still, it did not look angry. Miss Harmon's eyes were very blue, and her gaze was intense.

"I want to talk to you about *you*, Amanda," Miss Harmon said.

Amanda was startled. She felt like a bird in a tree, that has been seen.

"Amanda, so much of the time I look for you and you're not here."

"I'm always here," Amanda said. "I can't get sick even when I try. I never miss a day."

"Your body is here, but your mind isn't," Miss Harmon said. "Did you understand how Pamela and the others worked out the problem this morning?"

"Yes," Amanda said. "I just didn't get it done."

Should she say she missed the question because she was reading *The First Rider*? Probably it was better not to.

Miss Harmon glanced at Amanda's books on the floor.

"How far are you in *The First Rider*?" she asked.

"About half," Amanda said.

"I always liked that book," Miss Harmon said. "Even though the author missed one thing."

"What?" Amanda asked.

"A lot of the warriors in the Caucasus were women. Very likely a woman warrior captured the first horse."

Amanda tried to imagine a woman Zorak. It was, she

decided, imaginable. "Her name could have been Zorine," Amanda said.

"Could have been," Miss Harmon agreed. Amanda started feeling comfortable.

"When I was young," Miss Harmon said, "I never read *The First Rider* during geography class. I figured I would enjoy it more if I wasn't reading it when I was supposed to be doing something else."

Miss Harmon was silent. Amanda tried to figure out what she meant. Did she mean Amanda shouldn't read other books under her textbooks? She hadn't said so. She hadn't asked or told Amanda not to do it.

"Probably you were right," Amanda said. She mumbled quickly, "I won't read other books under my schoolbooks again."

Miss Harmon smiled. "Well, good," she said. "That's a very good decision you've reached. I think it will help you to do better with your schoolwork.

"Fiction books are so nice," Miss Harmon continued, "because, say, you read about Zorak, and it's inspiring that he—or maybe it was she—was so brave and dared to sacrifice an easy life, and you feel dizzy with him, and your feet hurt with him, and you almost get buried alive with him—"

"I haven't got to that part!" Amanda protested.

"—and yet when you put the book down you haven't

sacrificed, you're not dizzy, and your feet don't hurt at all. Of course, you don't have your own beautiful stallion, either."

"You told the end!" Amanda protested.

"I didn't, not really," Miss Harmon said firmly.

"Anyhow, the reason you people in fifth grade are sacrificing to learn arithmetic and other things is so you can have bigger lives and do more. Like Zorak. Or Zorine. Amanda, if you face the things you don't like, even things that scare you, they will change. Like arithmetic, for instance. It could become almost a friend. Not an easy friend, but a hard friend that challenges you. You can conquer arithmetic and a lot of other things, Amanda. You're smart."

"I'm average," Amanda said. "That's what my mother says." Amanda was going to say it nonchalantly, but somehow it didn't come out that way.

"Your mother told you that?" Miss Harmon said. She looked surprised.

"I heard her say it to somebody. On the phone," Amanda added.

"Well," Miss Harmon said, "she might be wrong."

"She never is," Amanda said.

"Even the smartest people are wrong sometimes," Miss Harmon persisted. "The way I see you, Amanda, is that you *are* smart, but you aren't putting your smartness to work. It would be good for you and for everybody if you did. Don't you think so?"

Amanda, not knowing what to say, tightened her Lyle Leveridge hand and muttered, "Maybe."

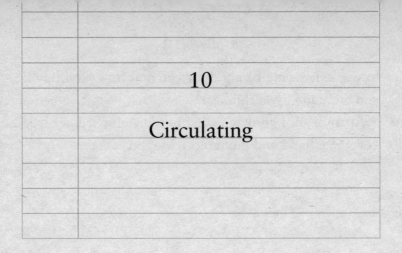

10

Circulating

Amanda sat cross-legged on her side of the bed. She wanted to tell Margaret about what had happened to her at school, but if she did, she was afraid Margaret would look down on her, so instead she just watched Margaret.

Margaret was working at her desk. It was bare except for Margaret's four-inch-thick wallet stuffed with signed snapshots of all her friends, and the book *How to Win Friends and Influence People,* by Dale Carnegie. Margaret had read the book at least three times and said it was very good.

Amanda had never read it, because it was a book that was so far beneath the Lone Ranger. He didn't have to care about winning friends: everybody just knew he was great and loved him for that and did what he said because he was right. He didn't have to try to influence anybody. It was weak to try to influence people, Amanda had always believed.

Margaret took two letters in white envelopes from her desk and read them, wrinkling her nose.

She got her pen, pink paper, a pink envelope, and the September 1954 issue of *Girl Talk* magazine.

"What are you doing?" Amanda asked, in her sweetest voice.

"Writing a letter," Margaret said.

"To that boy?" Amanda asked.

"To that boy," Margaret said, meaning, "Don't bother me."

Amanda got off the bed and stood up. She craned her neck so she could see the article Margaret was looking at. The headline said: "How to Let Him Down Gently."

Margaret started writing. Amanda moved closer. Margaret wrote, "Dear Henry." It looked as if she was copying everything she was writing straight out of *Girl Talk* magazine!

Amanda moved close enough to read the whole thing.

Dear Henry,
You are a very fine person and I have enjoyed knowing you, but since I am going steady now, I

cannot honorably write to you anymore. I am sure
some other girl will be perfect for you. I really would
not be.

> *Yours sincerely,*
> *Margaret Woods*

Amanda, looking over Margaret's shoulder and practically breathing down her neck, couldn't believe Margaret had let her get so close. It must be the luck from her clover!

Margaret said, "I let you read this because you are eleven years old, and it is time for you to start knowing about things. After next year I will be away at college, so if you are going to learn anything, I have to teach you now."

"How *can* you copy a letter instead of writing your own?" Amanda thought. "Why don't you want to write to Henry?" she asked.

"His letters are mushy and boring."

"But you told him a lie," Amanda said sternly. "You are not going steady."

Margaret turned around in her chair.

"You need to understand, Amanda, that when boys get to a certain age, their feelings are fragile. They look strong, but they are very weak. A girl has to protect them if she can."

"By telling a *lie*?"

Margaret explained. "Not to hurt a boy's feelings, it's all right to tell a lie. It is all right to tell a boy that you met another boy you like better. Because of the fragility of his ego, if he knew that just plain old reality is more interesting than he is, he would be devastated."

Amanda was astonished. Boys (like Bob Bostwick, the boy Margaret was currently dating) who looked strong as oxen were really writhing and squirming and trembling inside! It was amazing news—but also pleasing. Especially in the case of Bob Bostwick.

"It's true," Margaret insisted. "All the magazines say it. And anyway what I wrote isn't really a lie. I *am* going out with Bob Bostwick."

"Are you going to go steady with him?" Amanda asked.

"I don't know," Margaret said.

Amanda felt very bold and old. She said, "Are you *in love* with Bob Bostwick?"

"No, but he is a nice person," Margaret said.

Amanda didn't think he was a nice person but didn't say so. Bob Bostwick had a very short haircut, about a quarter inch long. His face looked as if it were made of boards, its expression changed so little—or else maybe it was made of flesh-colored cement. Whenever he saw Amanda he said, "Hi, Champ," and clamped his huge hand (he was a football fullback) over the top of her head. The Lone Ranger would have knocked his hand off immediately.

Amanda couldn't, because in the vicinity of Rome, Wisconsin, part of being polite was that if somebody else thought he was being nice when he wasn't, you just let it pass, even if it practically killed you.

"Do you *like* Bob Bostwick?" Amanda asked.

"Of course I like him. He is a very nice person."

"You just said that," Amanda said.

Margaret looked at her earnestly. "This is the main thing you need to understand, Amanda: when you are a teenager you have to circulate. Say you know someone is not the perfect person for you, but you go out with that person so you'll be with a whole bunch of people who see you circulating with that person, and then they think of you, but if you sat at home alone they would never think of you in a million years. But since you *are* out, one of them will think of you and want to take you away from the person you are circulating with."

Amanda made a face.

"You need to know these things, Amanda," Margaret said.

"But suppose somebody asks you out and you would rather stay home?"

"You should not 'rather stay home,' " Margaret said. "Only a drip would rather stay home."

Amanda bet the Lone Ranger sometimes would stay home. Amanda knew she would rather stay home and talk to Skipper than go out and circulate with someone she didn't like.

"Do you *kiss* him?" Amanda asked, getting her mind back on Bob Bostwick.

"You do kiss someone you circulate with, but not much," Margaret said.

"Why?"

"If they take you out and spend money on you, and they aren't rude, then you kiss them good night at the door."

"Even if you're just circulating with them?"

"*Yes!*" Margaret said. "At least, as long as they don't get too fresh."

"But what if you circulate and you keep on meeting somebody just like the last person you circulated with . . . and on and on, like that?" Amanda asked.

"That would never happen," Margaret said. But she didn't sound as certain as she usually did.

"Anyhow," she said, "I need to circulate. I have decided I am going to be a doctor and I need to know and understand all kinds of people—and there is no way a person is going to know them if she doesn't circulate."

Amanda was astonished. Margaret was a nurse's aide at North Wisconsin Hospital, but it had never occurred to Amanda that she would ever become a doctor.

"Why do you want to be a doctor?" Amanda asked.

"Because I will be good at it!" Margaret said, getting up to leave. "And besides, people are less phony when they are sick."

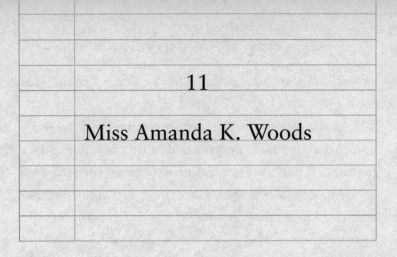

11

Miss Amanda K. Woods

Amanda sat on the bed, her mind rocking in the wake of Margaret's ambitions, like a little boat Margaret had left behind.

Amanda was depressed. She didn't want to become someone who circulated and wrote phony letters and had to become a doctor before she could be real. She didn't want to be herself, either. She wanted to be somebody else, somewhere else, but she didn't know who or where.

She opened the top drawer of Margaret's desk, telling herself she shouldn't, and looked at the cover of Margaret's leather-bound five-year diary to see if the key was in it. Margaret wrote pages and pages in her diary every night, and Amanda always wondered exactly what they said. If Margaret had left the key in it, it would be like saying, "Go ahead. Look!" But the key, as usual, was missing.

Amanda closed the drawer. She walked over to Margaret's dressing table and smelled Margaret's Tender Fire perfume. It had a wonderful smell of pine and gardenias and you could feel springtime in it growing like tiny flames. It didn't do much for Margaret, though, because Margaret never used enough.

Amanda put the glass perfume stopper back in the bottle. She glanced at her own five-year diary, sitting dusty on the bottom shelf of her bookcase with the key stuck in it. Probably Margaret had never even bothered to look at it.

On Christmas Day, when they got the diaries from their dad, Amanda had signed hers "Amanda K. Woods," in her fanciest handwriting in gold ink. But after that she hadn't been able to make herself write in it. Her normal handwriting was not good enough to keep up with the way she had written "Amanda K. Woods." Besides, everything interesting happened to Margaret, and nothing interesting happened to her.

The "K" in Amanda's name stood for "Karen." Both plain "Amanda Woods" and "Amanda Karen Woods" sounded like soft boneless names to Amanda. "Amanda K. Woods" had mystery and sharpness to it. The "K" was like having a sword in the middle of her name.

She wished somebody actually called her "Amanda K. Woods." She didn't want to wait all her life to be called it. She wanted it to happen before she got to be so old it didn't even matter.

If Lyle Leveridge had wanted his name changed, he would have thought of some way to do it, but Amanda couldn't think of any. She pressed her Lyle Leveridge hand against her forehead and thought.

If you had a pen pal, that person would have to call you whatever name you said you had, and in a magazine of Margaret's she'd seen an ad telling where a person could send away for an international pen pal. She picked up a stack of Margaret's magazines and started looking for it.

In just a few minutes she found it. She cut it out and filled it in with her interests—"sports, reading, horses"—and her address. On the top line she wrote: "Miss Amanda K. Woods," going over the "K." six times with ink.

The next day after school, she mailed it.

12

The Secret

Amanda was alone. She had forgotten she was Amanda K. Woods, and was just plain Amanda.

It was a bright, moonlit night. All the stores were closed in Rome, and there was no one on Main Street except one person moving quickly toward Amanda with an echoing *tap tap tap* of high-heeled shoes. At first Amanda couldn't see clearly who it was. And then she was sure it was her school principal, Miss Deverest, but something was odd about the shape of her face, and the furriness of her dress, and the way her pointy ears stuck up high on her head.

"Amanda," Miss Deverest growled, "it's a full moon at midnight, and, poor little girl, you're alone!" She grabbed Amanda's shoulders between her hairy paws.

"Miss Deverest," Amanda said, "excuse me—but you're a werewolf!"

Miss Deverest smiled the biggest smile Amanda had ever seen, and in the moonlight her long fangs gleamed.

"That's right," Miss Deverest said, "and that's why I know many things most people don't know. I know why not one single person likes you, Amanda. It's a secret. Shall I tell you?"

"No!" Amanda shouted.

Tears welled in Miss Deverest's brown eyes and trickled down her massive furry jaws. She looked lonely but not evil.

"Are you real?" Amanda asked.

Miss Deverest didn't answer that. The tears just kept running down her face.

"Shall I tell you the secret?" she repeated.

Amanda tried not to be afraid. "All right," she said. "Tell me!"

She never found out the secret, though, because right then she rolled hard into something warm and heavy that turned out to be Margaret, who woke up and was angry, but that didn't matter because there was no werewolf and Amanda wasn't on Main Street anymore.

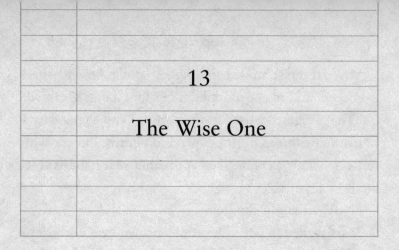

13

The Wise One

Margaret wrote an advice column for the Rome High School paper. A drawing of an owl wearing glasses was the logo for her column, and she signed it "The Wise One." As "The Wise One," Margaret always sounded much nicer and wiser than her normal self.

Margaret was leaning on pillows, reading her biology book and marking certain lines with a pencil. Amanda, next to her, was reading the first "Wise One" column of the year. For luck, she stretched her Lyle Leveridge hand behind her till for a second it just touched her four-leaf clover.

"This is a good column, Margaret," Amanda said.

"Thanks," Margaret said. She didn't look up.

"I know somebody with a problem that would be good for your column," Amanda said.

"Yeah, who?" Margaret said. She didn't sound grateful.

"There's a new girl at school," Amanda explained, "and she doesn't have any friends because people think she is stuck-up because of this other place she is from, and people don't trust her because she hasn't been around."

Margaret yawned. "A problem from Lincoln School won't do for the Rome High paper," she said.

Amanda got the sinking feeling that she would soon lose Margaret's attention.

"This girl is so troubled she is dreaming continually about werewolves!" Amanda said.

"Really?" Margaret sounded interested.

"Well, anyway, what should she do? Because I could tell her what you say. You are so good! You are probably the only person in town who can help her!" The Lone Ranger would not have been a flatterer, but Amanda felt she had no choice.

Margaret sat up. She put her book down.

"This girl needs to understand one simple thing," she said. "If she wants other people to be interested in her, she has to show interest in them. Also, she needs to understand human evolution."

"Human evolution!" Amanda said.

"It's like this," Margaret said. "From three million

years back—from the beginning of mankind—all people have lived in groups. Thousands and thousands of years later, they developed their brains.

"Groups of people are like herds of horses, or cows. They sniff the wind. They are alert for danger. They keep out strangers. They don't know why, they just do. And they all think as one. If one of them didn't, he or she would turn into a stranger.

"If this girl had just been snotty to one person, she could go to that person and apologize. But you say she was snotty to the entire group."

"I didn't say she was snotty," Amanda protested.

"It sounds to me like she was snotty," Margaret said. "If so, nothing she can say will ever make them trust her, because groups do not think in words and they do not decide things by listening to words. They decide by something else. This girl has to act like a cow or a horse or a fish.

"She has to pretend she has been at your school forever. She must stand around with all the girls who stand around, and listen to the conversation but not say one word. She should just look interested and friendly—that is *very* important—and look like she knows about everything that is going on.

"She should do this for weeks. Months, maybe. Finally, one day, someone in the group will make a mistake and talk to her."

"Why would anybody make a mistake?"

"Probably because her smell has changed. She will have been around them a long time—long enough to smell like the group."

Did the fifth-grade girls have a smell? Amanda didn't smell any smell on them at all. The boys didn't have any smell either.

"The fifth grade does not smell!" Amanda said.

"Everybody smells," Margaret said. "The smell is sub-liminal. You smell it even though you don't know you're smelling it. Like the hidden pictures in advertisements. You don't know you're seeing them, but they affect you anyway."

It was astonishing the things Margaret knew. Amanda tried to remember all the information.

"Then what? After she smells okay and somebody talks to her, then what?"

"Then she can answer."

"What should she say?"

"She should just respond to what is said. The important thing isn't what she says back. It's the way she acts. This is *crucial*. She shouldn't act surprised, or startled, or anything like that. Absolutely *the worst* thing she could do would be to act thrilled. She has to answer just as if the other girls have been talking to her for years and years, and it is normal. But the answer should be short.

"After that she can say a few things—but no more

than one sentence once or twice a week. She shouldn't say anything about where she's from. That will just make them remember that she is stuck-up. She should ask the other girls about themselves. As Dale Carnegie says, people like you when you are interested in their interests. But what she asks shouldn't be too personal. For example, she could ask them if they like Pat Boone."

Pat Boone was a singer on TV. Amanda didn't like Pat Boone. When he sang he smiled all the time, even in the serious parts.

"I don't like Pat Boone," Amanda said. "He looks like his lips are melting and running off his face."

"What does it matter what *you* like? It doesn't even matter what *she* likes. If she doesn't like Pat Boone, she should never say it. That will just make people think she is stuck-up. She should say, 'Do you like Pat Boone?' and then just listen to what the other people say."

Amanda frowned. She couldn't help it. What if everybody really hated Pat Boone, but they all said they liked him just to fit what they thought everybody else thought? Everybody would be cowards, tricking everybody else and themselves, too, and the group would be nothing but fake.

"Or," Margaret went on, "if she doesn't want to talk about Pat Boone, she can ask somebody a question. People always like to talk about themselves. That's what

Dale Carnegie says. Then in about a month, she can invite the person who is the friendliest to do something with her."

"Like what?"

"Whatever kids do in grade school. I don't remember! Go to a movie. Skate. Something like that." Margaret opened her biology book, then closed it. Once she had started being the Wise One, it was hard to quit.

"Where is this girl from?"

"Out West."

" 'Out West,' " the Wise One mocked. "Don't you even keep track of states?"

"Montana, I think," Amanda said.

"What's this girl's name?" the Wise One asked.

"Elizabeth."

"Elizabeth! Aha!" said the Wise One triumphantly. "A name like Elizabeth. That could be part of the problem. She could—when they start talking to her—say she wants to be called Beth or Liz. That might help." She opened her biology book again.

"Thank you, Margaret, I'll give her your advice," Amanda said.

Amanda was in Skipper's pasture. Instead of forking hay to Skipper, she carried a small bunch of it to him in her hands.

When she got close to him, she half shrugged, half bowed and laid the hay at his feet.

"Just call me Mandy," she said. She widened her eyes and lifted the corners of her mouth so it would show no trace of moping.

Then she went back for another bunch. Skipper was still eating when she threw this one at his feet. He pricked his ears the way he did when he didn't know what she was up to.

"You kids can call me Mandy," Amanda said. She smiled like Pat Boone. Skipper snorted and tossed his head.

Amanda brought a third bunch of hay. Skipper didn't want it. Amanda puzzled him. He watched her with concerned eyes.

"Hey, why don't you guys call me Mandy? I wish you guys would call me Mandy," Amanda said.

Skipper ambled away.

"Skipper, come back!" Amanda said.

Amanda actually hated the name Mandy. Skipper could tell.

Even for belonging, there were some things a person did not do.

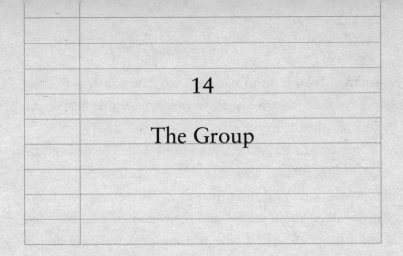

14

The Group

Amanda always found a place to stand that was as far as possible from Mary Jane Stoltenberg. Even so, it was very difficult for Amanda to stand around with the fifth-grade girls at recess. They pretended not to see her. She wanted to say something, anything, so that they would admit she was there. Keeping silent was the hardest thing she had ever done, and all the time she kept wanting to walk away. Or run.

To keep from running away, she thought of Lyle Leveridge, who wasn't scared of anything. She thought of how she had his hand, and he had hers. She thought how she was really Amanda *K.* Woods, a person with a sword in the middle of her name. She thought how she had a four-leaf clover and possibly a letter coming to her soon from a foreign country, and how, deep down, she was smart. Miss Harmon had said so. Amanda was not the person the fifth-grade girls were seeing. Inside herself she was another, better person.

For fifteen days Amanda stood with the fifth-grade girls at recess and nobody said one word to her.

It was a painful time. Just as if she weren't there, the girls talked about school and their families, and watched the fifth-grade boys. The fifth-grade boys were acting different from the way they used to, so they were worth watching.

One day David Johnson, who was the Lutheran minister's son and very smart and serious, chased Bob Larson with a dead mouse that he was holding by the tail. Both boys practically ran into the girls, who were disgusted. None of them could believe David could do anything so childish. The fifth-grade girls all agreed that the fifth-grade boys had deteriorated and were much, much worse and more revolting than they had ever been.

Another day Pamela Collins told everybody that she was starting to hate the name Pamela and would everyone call her Pam.

One afternoon Mary Jane Stoltenberg actually told a joke. She asked, "Do you know why Lincoln School teachers don't smile?"

Nobody knew.

"Because, if they want to give a class a smile, first they

have to get it from the supply room with a form signed by Miss Deverest. And she usually won't sign, so the old smiles get all musty in there."

"Do you know why Miss Harmon can smile anytime?" Pam Collins said.

Nobody knew.

"Because she was afraid there'd be a smile shortage in Rome, so she brought a big suitcase with her from California. She keeps it under her bed, and inside it she keeps a million smiles."

One morning Monica Rogowski told about how to get free chocolate. Her cousin in Manitowoc had done it.

What you did was buy a chocolate bar at the grocery store, eat it, and save the wrapper. Then you wrote to the company that made it. You said that you had bought a chocolate bar, but that when you opened it, instead of being all brown, it had white spots! You enclosed the wrapper from your chocolate bar and put your full return address on the envelope.

In a few weeks, Monica said, the candy company would send you a complete box of thirty-six chocolate bars, with apologies for the white one. They would explain that chocolate changes color when it gets old or a store is too hot, but that it doesn't go bad, and they would ask for the name of the store that had sold you the white-spotted chocolate bar, because that store should have taken the white-spotted chocolate bar off their shelves when it passed a certain date, and they wanted to remind the store about that.

"A person couldn't do that here," Sheri Anderson said.

Everybody knew a person couldn't. There were only two groceries in Rome, and their owners knew most everybody's parents. If you made a false complaint about a store, your parents would find out and you would get punished.

"That's something a person shouldn't do anyway," Pam Collins said. "If the chocolate bar didn't turn white, it would really be stealing." She turned to Monica. "I don't mean your cousin is a thief, I know it's just a game—but it's not honest."

A stillness went through the group. Amanda could feel it. She respected Pam Collins for telling the truth. It was not easy to do in a group.

It was Pam Collins who was the first person in the group who spoke to Amanda. She did it just as if she had been speaking to Amanda all her life. She was standing next to Amanda during recess and said, "I wish I had a horse. I still remember what you wrote about yours."

"I liked what you wrote about singing, too," Amanda said, and then—following the Wise One's advice—she did not say a word in the group for three more days.

When she did open her mouth again, everybody in the

group turned to look at her, but she kept going very calmly. She said to Pam Collins, "What's it like to have twin brothers? Yours are so cute."

She expected Pam Collins to talk about them the way Margaret talked about her, to say they were pests. But Pam Collins agreed her brothers were cute, in fact she said she adored them.

One day Amanda decided to invite Pam Collins to do something. She saw her alone, leaving school.

"Would-you-like-to-go-to-my-dad's-hotel-and-have-some-ice-cream—well-I-suppose-not?" was the way Amanda put it, squeezing together the fingers of her Lyle Leveridge hand.

"Would you repeat that?" Pam Collins said.

Amanda repeated it, except for the last part.

Pam Collins said sure.

15

Party in Room 17

Pam Collins had curly black hair and blue eyes, and so did her two little first-grade brothers, Max and Markie. Amanda thought all three of them were the most beautiful people she had ever seen and that having twin brothers was the most special thing in the world.

Pam was one of the best students in fifth grade. She was definitely the best singer. Whenever the school put on a play, Pam got solo singing roles. Amanda admired this; nobody in her family could sing at all.

When they got to the Rome Hotel, Amanda first took Pam into her dad's office and introduced her. Then she introduced Pam to Charley, the cook for the Loggers' Inn. She thought the ice cream servings might be better that way.

"Wow!" said Pam Collins when she saw the Loggers'

Inn. She went around the room looking at all the logging tools and photos. Then Amanda showed her the player piano in the bar, and they played old songs, their feet pushing the pedals that moved the piano roll.

After that they sat down in the Loggers' Inn, and Charley sent out maple-nut ice cream with double helpings of chocolate sauce on top.

"My family has always wanted to come in here," Pam said. "We just never did."

"I come here every day," Amanda said. "Usually I do my homework here."

"That's nice," Pam said. "I do mine at home on the kitchen table. But it's hard to concentrate sometimes with Max and Markie around."

"You could do it here with me," Amanda said. She hesitated. "If you ever wanted to."

And Pam said, if her mother let her, she would.

After that, Amanda and Pam walked together down to the hotel almost every day and studied. One day they got a surprise, because when they arrived, Miss Harmon was there already, talking to Amanda's father and telling him how wonderful it was that he was keeping history alive through the Rome Hotel. Amanda hoped they hadn't also been talking about her.

That night on the way home, Amanda's dad asked her how her arithmetic was.

"So-so," Amanda said.

"I'll make a bargain with you," he said.

"What kind of bargain?" Amanda asked.

"If you can get straight 100s on your arithmetic, so long as the hotel isn't full, you and your friend can have a room of your own to study in."

Amanda thought about it. She was excited, but she tried not to show it.

"I'll see if Pam is interested," she said. There wasn't any point in making such a sacrifice for arithmetic, if there was no reason.

When Amanda told Pam the next day, she said, "Let's go look at the room." That afternoon Amanda's dad took them up to it and opened the door, and they knew they wanted it. It was Room 17, the tower room with a view of most of Rome and the Red Cedar River.

It was round, with a bay window, and had a desk that was curved on one side and fitted in under the window. When Amanda's dad brought in an extra desk chair, they could see that the desk was big enough for both of them to use. The room also had a bed and two wicker rocking chairs, with soft cushions.

"I'll give you two free trial days," Amanda's dad said, smiling. After that, to keep on staying, Amanda would have to show him every single arithmetic paper. That was the hard part.

"What do you get on your arithmetic?" Amanda asked Pam, after her dad had left.

"Straight hundreds, almost," Pam said.

"How do you do it?"

"I check every single problem twice," Pam said.

"I hoped there was an easier way," Amanda said.

In terms of homework, Amanda was a scrambler. She probably had always done homework the fastest of anybody in her class. Grab it and go was her method. Afterward, never bring the corrected homework back home, where it might attract unfavorable attention.

Pam Collins was very different. She was a person gathered together in her ways. She kept her books beside her in the exact order in which she intended to do her homework, and then at a regular, careful pace she did it all until she finished it. You could read every word or number Pam Collins wrote without having to puzzle it out. Also, if Pam Collins wrote that 2018 divided by 37 was 54.54, you could be sure that was the true answer.

To keep Room 17, Amanda also had to get the true answers. Pam would not share hers.

The fifth grade was doing long division with decimals, and getting everything right took time. Amanda decided that since she had to do it right, she might as well also make it neat. When she finished it all, she double-checked it. There were four problems with mistakes, and Amanda fixed them.

One part of her, even with Pam working beside her, thought the whole thing was very boring. Another part of her considered the idea that a wrong answer in arithmetic was a kind of lie. Every time you got a wrong answer and let it stay, you were letting yourself be a person who didn't care about the truth.

With her neat numbers and new correct double-checked arithmetic, her paper actually looked pretty. Amanda was proud of it. At the top of it she wrote the date and not just her usual "Amanda Woods" but "Amanda K. Woods."

Amanda Woods was the kind of person who would get her arithmetic more or less right at least half the time. Amanda K. Woods was, like Pam Collins, the kind of person who didn't tell a lie. What she said, even on a homework paper, you could count on to be true.

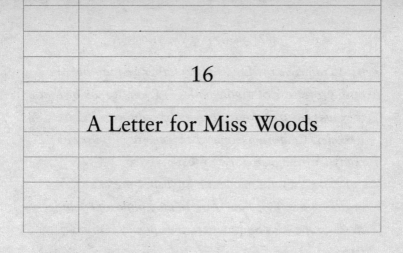

16

A Letter for Miss Woods

The sky-blue envelope was so fine and smooth that Amanda thought it might dissolve in her hand. The handwriting on it flowed like blue silk thread. Elegantly and loosely knotted, it formed Amanda's real name exactly the way it was supposed to be written. Even in her own fanciest script, Amanda had never seen "Amanda K. Woods" look so good.

With great care, using her mother's silver paper knife and her Lyle Leveridge hand, she cut the envelope.

> *Lyon, France*
> *2 October 1954*

Dear Miss Woods,

I am a French student, age of 17. I study English in school. My parents say I must have an American pen pal to improve my English. My father and mother are both professors of Mathematics in Lyon. It may be that they will teach at the University of California in Berkeley, California, some year. They say I must be ready with English if we go there.

Really, I do not much like English. I prefer soccer or do you say foot-ball? Also I enjoy philosophy and to ski in the Alps and to go to the cinema with my friends.

What are your hobbies, Miss Woods? Please write me. I will write back. If I do not write letters in English, my father will put himself in anger and kill me.

Sincerely,

Antoine Bonnier

P.S. I enclose, my photo. My name, in case you wouldn't know, is pronounced "An-twahn Bone-yea."

Amanda studied Antoine Bonnier's photo. He had a nice smile, a slightly narrow face, wavy hair combed straight back, and eyes that looked as if they were trying to see deep into things. Except for the eyes, he could have been a friend of Margaret's.

Amanda loved the way he looked, and his handwriting, which was truly like the handwriting of a prince or someone like that. Anyway, not like the handwriting of someone from Rome, Wisconsin.

Amanda decided to write him at once—after gathering herself together, the way Pam would have done.

She tried to remember all she knew about France. The information wavered before her mind's eye like a landscape seen distorted and shimmering with distant heat.

France: at some time, around two hundred years back, France had helped the United States to fight their revolution for freedom from England.

At one time, Amanda didn't know exactly when, France had a queen. Her name was Marie Antoinette. Her husband's name was King somebody with Roman numerals after it.

The two of them lived very well, while the poor people of their country went hungry. Someone told the queen the people had no bread, but she only laughed and said, "Let them eat cake."

The poor people and even the middle-class people got very angry and invented an instrument called the guillotine. This was like a paper cutter, but much, much bigger. They used it to cut off the king's and queen's heads. That began the French Revolution, when the French got rid of kings and queens entirely, as well as a whole bunch of other people.

The French invented French bread, but they didn't invent french fries or French vanilla ice cream. Those, Amanda's mother had told her, were invented in Chicago.

No matter what Antoine said about his father killing him, Amanda was afraid he wouldn't write back to her unless he thought she was seventeen. She had to write a letter that sounded adult.

Luckily it was a Saturday, and Margaret was over at a friend's house. That gave Amanda a chance to use Margaret's desk.

She addressed an envelope with her very best "Amanda K. Woods" on the return address corner. She pushed Margaret's stuff to the side of Margaret's desk so she could type the letter on Margaret's typewriter.

> *Dear Antoine,*
>
> *I am glad to hear from you. You may call me Amanda, although please always use Amanda K. Woods on the envelope. My family is my father, he owns a hotel in Rome, Wisconsin; my mother; and my sister, Margaret, who is sometimes a pain in the neck, but I think she will grow up someday.*
>
> *In school the subjects I like are English, Social Studies, and sometimes Science. I am, sometimes, an "A" student.*
>
> *I like to swim, ski, snowshoe, go to movies, and ride horseback. My horse's name is Skipper.*
>
> *I do not know very much about France, however, I thank you for helping with our Revolution. I am sorry*

*about yours. I hope you didn't lose anyone in your
family.*

*The queen was wrong, cake is only good from time
to time. Someday I would like to have a philosophy of
life but it is very hard to get one around here.*

*Do please write back! I will gladly help you with
your English. I am an expert at it and have spoken it
all my life.*

Sincerely,

Amanda K. Woods

Amanda wanted to send a photo of herself, but she
didn't have a single good one. The best one she could
find, in a jumbled box of snapshots in the living room,
was of her and her dad in their boat. Just looking at the
photo, she could remember the wind in her face and
the boat going at top speed, almost skipping over the
waves.

It was too bad that the photo was blurred and that,
even though her hair covered part of her face, she didn't
look seventeen.

It wasn't fair. It wasn't fair, because Margaret had a
new, very, very good photo of herself in a hundred small-
sized prints for all her best friends, sitting right on the
corner of the desk.

Amanda picked up one of them. It wasn't just a regular snapshot, it was Margaret's senior portrait, and she had posed two hours at Schilling's Studio to get it.

Amanda had always thought that Margaret was ordinary-looking, sort of pretty when she took out her curlers and cleaned off her suntan lotion. In her senior portrait, though, she was beautiful.

She looked out levelly, straight ahead—not with her head dipped down or to the side in a teasing look, the way some other senior girls were photographed. She was wearing a simple, sleeveless black velvet dress with a delicate gauze-net panel in front. Her hair was sleek, in a perfect pageboy that framed her face. Her lips curved upward, not smiling really, but warm and confident.

She looked like the person you would want for your best friend. She looked like a person who was saying inside, "I am beautiful and I am going to be a doctor."

Could it be that you could never really see your own family, the people closest to you, until you saw someone else's picture of them?

In the photo Margaret was a stranger, stronger than Wonder Woman, truly the Wise One, more real and more beautiful than a movie star.

Anybody would write to the girl in that photo. Quickly Amanda enclosed one in her letter to Antoine.

17

Secrets of Room 17

The days got shorter. The homework got longer. When the girls finished, they would look out the bay window at Main Street, to the city park with its carpet of fallen leaves and its pretty blue-and-white bandstand, and beyond to the fast-flowing, not yet frozen Red Cedar River.

Sometimes, when they finished early, they would pick up the phone in Room 17 and call down for ice cream from room service.

Lots of times it was Charley the cook who brought it up to them, on a silver tray, in tall glasses with extra-long spoons, and asked them how their work was going.

After he left, they would tell each other things.

Amanda told Pam how much she liked fishing with her dad.

Pam said wistfully, "I wish my dad and I spent time together." Her dad was a truck driver, and he had to be away from home a lot, sometimes for two weeks straight. She wished her dad didn't drive trucks.

"I miss him a lot," she said. "Sometimes I'm afraid that he'll get in an accident on the highway. Once I even dreamed it."

"Just because you dream something, that doesn't mean it will come true," Amanda said. (She knew. If dreams came true, Miss Deverest would probably have turned her into a werewolf.)

"I know dreams usually don't happen," Pam said. "I just wish I saw him all the time, and we were really close, like you and your dad."

Amanda felt funny. She felt all of a sudden that she wasn't quite telling the truth about herself and her dad.

"I see my dad," Amanda said, "I see him every day. But we aren't that close. I can't talk to him. I mean, we talk about fishing, or he shows me how to swim better— but I can't talk about anything personal with him."

"Why?" Pam said.

"I don't know," Amanda said. "My dad is a person who doesn't want to talk. I don't know why."

"And he seems so friendly!" Pam said. "You should make him talk to you. Maybe you have to teach him to do it."

"Me teach my dad!" Amanda said.

"If he can teach you things, why can't you teach him?" Pam asked.

"Parents teach kids," Amanda said. "Kids don't teach parents."

"But they can," Pam insisted.

"If I try to change my dad, it might make him angry," Amanda said.

"Maybe," Pam said, "but then again it might make him glad."

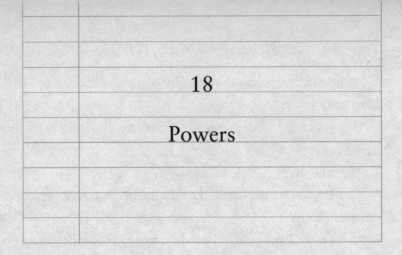

18

Powers

Amanda was sitting on the bed reading an interesting book from the library. It was called *Yoga: Pathway to Health and Knowledge.*

The author was Swami Savananda. Mr. Savananda was a yogi. Yogis were people who did yoga exercises. According to the book, the exercises were the way to health, and to developing powers higher than most people knew they had.

Amanda leafed through the book, looking at photos of the author doing the exercises. He was a young, calm-looking, rather hairy man with extraordinarily large eyes, dressed in a swimming suit. In some exercises, he was upside down with his legs knotted up in various ways that looked as if they could never come unknotted, while his large eyes seemed to say, "I know exactly how to get out of this. In my mind, I am already out."

Amanda looked for a picture of the swami kissing his elbow. There wasn't one.

She turned more pages. She got to a part where Swami Savananda said that some very advanced yogis could even foresee the future. They had developed an organ called the "Third Eye," which was not a physical eye but rather a little indentation right above the bridge of the nose, midway between a person's actual eyes.

Amanda felt for the indentation. Sure enough, it was there. She rubbed it with her Lyle Leveridge hand.

Margaret, looking up from her homework, said, "What *are* you doing?"

"Developing special powers," Amanda said.

"Special powers!" Margaret mocked. "Tell me, how's your friend from Montana?"

"Who?" Amanda said.

"Elizabeth," Margaret reminded her, and Amanda remembered.

"Your advice was really working great, Margaret," Amanda said, "but then, a few weeks ago, just after somebody spoke to Liz for the first time, she and her whole family moved away."

"She should be all right anywhere now," Margaret said. "She knows the method."

Margaret reached into her desk drawer and pulled out an empty picture frame. Then she took a photo out of her purse, and forced it under the glass. She set the framed picture on her dresser. Amanda's thumb on her third eye pretty much blocked her two regular eyes, but still she could see whose picture was in the frame. Her thumb dropped.

"Oh no!" Amanda cried. "Not Bob Bostwick!"

"I'm going out with him a lot, and he gave it to me," Margaret said.

So as not to see the face of Bob Bostwick, Amanda rubbed her third eye more. She felt she might be attaining powers.

"You should not put that photo up there, Margaret," Amanda said, "because, because . . ." The why would not come to her.

Margaret ignored her.

Amanda rubbed her third eye again with her Lyle Leveridge hand. She tried to contact a knowledge of the future. She felt headachey. Maybe that was a sign of success.

"Are you going out with him again tonight?" Amanda asked.

"Yes," Margaret said.

"You shouldn't do it," Amanda said. "You *really* shouldn't do it. Something bad will happen if you do."

"Like what?" Margaret said.

"I don't know exactly, but you should break your date," Amanda said.

"Amanda, mind your own business!" Margaret said.

It was seven when Bob Bostwick came by, shaking Amanda's parents' hands, pulling Amanda's ponytail, and taking Margaret away.

It must have been very late, Amanda never really knew how late, when she felt the jolt of Margaret's body dropping on their bed. There was a smell of mud in the room. Amanda reached out in the darkness and touched her sister's arm. It was cold and trembling.

"What's the matter with you?" Amanda demanded.

"Nerves," Margaret said.

Nerves were very bad. Nerves were something only their mother had.

Margaret breathed out a long, slow breath. "Bob landed his car in the Red Cedar tonight," she said.

"In the river?" Amanda said.

"He drove really fast and spun out on a curve. He does it all the time for the thrill. But this time he spun too far. The car almost rolled over. We just missed a tree."

Margaret breathed out another long breath and shivered. "I couldn't get the car door open, but Bob got his and mine open. The river wasn't deep, but it was slippery. I fell. The water was cold! A guy had to tow Bob's car. I got a taxi here from Rome—but don't you *ever* tell Mother and Daddy!"

"I promise. I won't," Amanda whispered.

Without turning on the light, Amanda got up and felt her way to the bathroom. She brought a towel back for Margaret.

In the darkness there were squishy sounds as Margaret pulled off her wet shoes. Then she stood up and turned on the light, blinding Amanda, and pitched something into the wastebasket by the bed.

Amanda's eyes adjusted and she peered down into the wastebasket. The photo of Bob Bostwick was in it, frame and all.

Margaret undressed. She put on a long flannel granny-style nightgown instead of her usual baby-doll pajamas. She got into bed and snapped off the light.

"What I don't understand is, you knew it was going to happen," Margaret whispered. "So tell me: *how* did you know?"

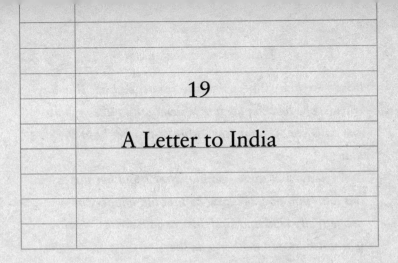

19

A Letter to India

It was strange to think of writing to a swami, but a person who could write a letter to France could just as well write one to India, too.

Amanda found the address of Swami Savananda's publisher in his book. Then she gathered her thoughts and wrote.

Dear Swami Savananda,

I have read (partly) your book Yoga: Pathway to Health and Vision. *After I read it I started rubbing my Third Eye. Then I got an insight that my sister shouldn't go out with her boyfriend, and I told her so.*

My sister, Margaret, is 17. Her boyfriend is a creep, 18, named Bob Bostwick, who pulls my hair. I don't see why when my sister is so popular and smart (or at least everybody thinks *she is so smart) and has so many friends, she had to pick a boyfriend who pulls my hair and calls me "Champ" or "Muscle-Bound," but she did.*

Anyway, that same evening, after I told her not to go out with him or something bad would happen, he drove really wild and sunk his car in the river, but he was not hurt and neither was she.

What I want to know is, could I really have foreseen this accident because I rubbed my Third Eye? Also, is it possible that by telling her something bad would happen, I made it happen? I do not always like my sister but I didn't mean to hurt her.

Very truly yours,

Amanda K. Woods

P.S. Please write back at once.

Despite her urgent request, he didn't.

20

Charley's Story

December and real winter came.

Times when Pam had to stay home with Max and Markie, Amanda did her homework at a table in the Loggers' Inn. If her father wasn't around, she went back into the kitchen to talk to Charley, whose father had actually been a logging camp cook. He told her stories of the logging days, and then, one afternoon, he asked her if she knew how her mother and father met.

Amanda didn't.

"Well, I met your mother first," Charley said, leaning his elbow against the open window where he passed food out to the dining room. "She came in here looking for a job, it was her first job after college, and I hired her right off. So pretty she was, and young. Like Margaret, but even prettier.

"Her first day on the job, the whole place was full of people. It was so hot down in Chicago that all those city folks moved out. Seemed like half of them was right here, in this dining room.

"Your mother never had waited on people before, and she forgot which table got which food, also she messed up the adding on the checks, and pretty soon everything was all balled up, and she got very nervous and spilled a glass of iced tea over a lady's dress, and her own waitress uniform. She ran and brought the lady all the napkins from a table where people were just sitting down, and then she started to cry, right there, so I just led her back into the kitchen and said, 'Look honey, this isn't the work for you.' And right then was when your father walked in, and he said your mom looked like she *could* be good at bookkeeping, so he persuaded his dad to keep her on, and that was that. Your dad can get kind of cross, but he was sweet that day, the way he rescued her."

"This isn't what I want to hear about my mother!" Amanda thought. Her mother had been clumsy! Her mother hadn't always done everything right! The whole story made Amanda very angry, because according to her mother, Amanda was always supposed to do everything right or she was very terrible, but yet, according to Charley, her mother wasn't perfect, either.

It could have been a romantic story, except for that.

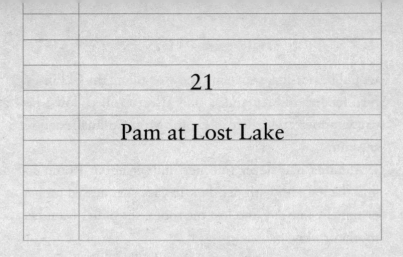

21

Pam at Lost Lake

On days when there wasn't homework, Amanda and Pam went ice-skating with a bunch of other girls at the Rome Skating Rink. One time Mary Jane Stoltenberg was there and Amanda accidentally skated into her. Amanda was scared when she saw who she was crashing toward, but Mary Jane put out her arms to stop Amanda so they didn't fall, and then smiled and said, "Hello!"

Sometimes Amanda and Pam took Max and Markie in their thick padded snowsuits and helped them learn to skate. The little boys' cheeks and noses got very red from the winter air, but they would never admit they were cold, and when they fell down they laughed and laughed as if it was the biggest joke in the world.

On the very cold days, Amanda's dad always gave Pam a ride home from the hotel. Sometimes Pam's mother would be outside, shoveling snow or filling the Collinses' bird feeder, and Amanda's dad always rolled down his car window and called, "Hello, Mrs. Collins! Nice to see you."

Amanda had never told her mother about Room 17 and the bargain with her dad. In case she messed up her arithmetic one day and lost the room, she didn't want her mother to know.

She had figured her father would tell her mother, anyway, but he must not have. When Amanda showed her mother her report card with an A+ in arithmetic, her mother was amazed. "Amanda!" she said. "Wonders never cease!"

Right then Amanda asked her mother if Pam could spend the weekend at Lost Lake. "Pam's really nice, and she's almost a professional singer," Amanda said.

"For doing so well in arithmetic, you deserve a treat," Amanda's mother said, and she agreed that Pam could visit.

The first thing Margaret said about Amanda's friend staying over was "Don't you two touch my stuff!"

But then she said, "It's nice you have a friend coming. I'll sleep in the living room so you can be alone with her."

Pamela rode out with Amanda and her dad on the Thursday when Christmas vacation started. Amanda was nervous about the visit, but it turned out to be one of the best times Amanda had ever had in her life.

On Friday, which wasn't too cold, they rode double on Skipper. When they came back, they combed his long and shaggy winter coat.

Amanda pointed out to Pam where all the grass snakes were hibernating. She told Pam she was sorry she couldn't show her how to catch grass snakes behind the head and hold them, because it was fun to look in their eyes while their angry red tongues flickered softly against your finger.

Pamela said it was enough to hear about it.

Amanda took Pam to see the pheasants.

The pheasants, seven of them, had settled in the back of Skipper's pasture between sheltering pines. Amanda's father had laid down straw all around there and made it like a pheasant living room. He had bought a fifty-pound bag of corn especially for the birds.

Amanda and Pam threw the pheasants corn. They were as tame as chickens and didn't fly away. With their iridescent green necks and shining red breasts, they strutted around in the straw fearless and proud, like kings.

"They're like Cool Whiskers," Pam said. Cool Whiskers was Pam's cat.

"How?" Amanda asked.

"They walk around always sure that they deserve the

best. They never question why food comes, or wonder if they're worth it. They just think, 'I am beautiful. I *am* the best. It is a privilege for the whole world to serve me.' "

Pam laughed. "Maybe animals that think like that convince us it's true."

Amanda thought of Margaret and her mother, who always seemed sure they were the best. But the pheasants were more like Lyle. He always figured he *could* be best, but he never made other people feel they weren't.

For the entire three days of Pam's visit, Amanda's mother cooked especially delicious meals. The only awkward time came late Friday night. Amanda and Pam were sitting in the living room with Amanda's mother and dad. Her dad was being nice. When he got himself a scotch and her mother a martini, he asked Amanda and Pam if they wanted Cokes. Instead of reading the newspaper, he actually listened to the conversation. As she sipped her martini, Amanda's mother explained to Pam how she had once wanted to be an actress.

"If you want to be a professional performer," she advised, "you should have your parents take you to the opera in Minneapolis."

"I'd like that," Pam said.

"Amanda says you're a very good singer," Amanda's mother said praisingly.

"I'm learning," Pam said.

"Why don't you sing for us? Step over in front of the fireplace. That can be your stage." Amanda's mother sounded very, very warm and friendly.

Pam looked uncertain.

"Sing for us! We'd like to hear how good you are!" Amanda's mother smiled. She held up her engraved silver cigarette holder like a conductor's baton, and her red lipstick reflected the orange light of the fire. She looked commanding and glamorous and beautiful, like the actress she had wanted to be.

"I'd be happy to some other time, Mrs. Woods," Pam said.

Amanda felt let down. Her mother said, "Just one song for us! What you do best—"

Amanda's father said, "Pam looks tired. I think the girls should go along to bed. They'll be talking half the night anyway."

Pam didn't look tired! Amanda's dad was killing the chance for them to hear Pam! Amanda hoped she would say she wasn't tired and would sing. But Pam said, "You're right, I really am tired, Mr. Woods," and so both Amanda and Pam said good night.

In the bedroom they looked at all the pictures of Margaret on the bulletin board, and then Pam asked to look at photos of Amanda, and Amanda slipped out into the living room and got them.

Her father was hidden behind his paper, and her mother's face had lost its vivacity. She sipped her drink as if she were sitting alone. If only Pam had sung, Amanda thought. And Pam wasn't even tired!

But then, when she showed Pam her pictures, explaining them took her mind off the lost moment.

Saturday, Amanda showed Pam a sport she had invented herself. She called it "sliding the spruces." She had asked Pamela to bring heavy gloves and old pants and jacket and scarf to do it.

On Saturday morning they put on their heavy clothes and snowshoed across frozen and snow-drifted Lost Lake to the island. There Amanda led the way to the spruces. They looked black and gloomy from her house, but up close, Amanda had found, they were bright green and a shelter from the wind.

Amanda and Pam took off their snowshoes and brushed snow from their clothes.

"Now look! Watch this!" Amanda called, and she began to climb the tallest of the spruces. Its dense branches were slender and limber and in places sticky with sap. Amanda held on near the trunk and climbed toward the top until the branches became almost too weak to hold her.

"Be careful!" Pam called.

"I'm okay. This is the way!" Amanda yelled, and let go

and began sliding on a cushion of branches that bent under her and held her, all the way to the ground.

"Neat!" Pam said. "It's a living slide!" And she started climbing.

They did it over and over again, for half the afternoon, until the sun was dropping in the west. Then Pam said, "I feel like singing."

She stood between the spruces facing the western sun and sang "Stranger in Paradise" and then "It's Only a Paper Moon." After that she sang "Hello Young Lovers" and "We Kiss in a Shadow," from *The King and I.*

Amanda listened, loving the music and the words and the emotion, wondering how so much richness of sound could come from one small person.

Pam finished. She caught her breath and stamped her feet to get the cold out of them.

"You are wonderful!" Amanda said. "I wish you would have sung for my folks!"

Pam looked at Amanda curiously. "Your mother didn't want me to sing. Didn't you know that?"

Amanda was astounded. "Yes she did! She asked you three times!"

"She asked me—more, she dared me," Pam said. "But she didn't want me to sing."

"That's crazy!" Amanda said.

"I could tell from the way she was sitting and the way

she looked that she didn't really want me to. Your dad did, but your mom didn't."

"But he said for us to go to bed! He didn't even say once that you should sing!"

"He wanted me to, but he knew it was a bad idea," Pam said.

"But why?"

"Because your mother didn't want me to sing."

"But why?"

"I don't know," Pam said.

Amanda didn't understand how two people—she and Pam—could be in the same place at the same time and see what happened completely opposite. One of them must be crazy!

"Anyhow," she said, "I'm glad you sang now. I loved it."

"Should I sing one more?" Pam said. Amanda nodded, and Pam sang "Some Enchanted Evening," her voice stretching out across Lost Lake, rising toward the red-orange sunset like a banner.

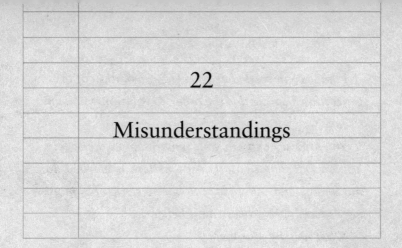

22

Misunderstandings

> Lyon
> 14 December

Dear Amanda,

Thank you for your letter and photo. You have the air very beautiful and also intelligent.

I never expected to have a pen friend who is so attractive!

It is very kind of you and it is very impressing that you follow the news in France and worry about my family. We all go well! I believe you Americans call almost anything a revolution. Really, this was not what we French would call a revolution—only a small riot. Some Frenchmen do not want to give up all of Indochina or even Vietnam and never, the glory of Empire.

I am very interested at your U.S. revolution of the generation Beat. Is this the other Revolution you want to say?

You are very witty in your remark about the cake! You are referring to Marie Antoinette? Or maybe I do not understand. Amanda, you have a sense of humour very special, very American, I believe.

What new in your life?

Nothing is new in my life apart the riot. (My lip was cut but it is healing.)

I would like to give you a good hit of telephone, but, sorry, I cannot, it would be very expensive.

Sincerely,

Antoine

P.S. What, please, are "movies"?

Amanda didn't know what a hit of telephone was. She didn't know what the generation Beat was. She had to ask Margaret. Margaret said it was "The Beat Generation," a movement to change American society.

She showed Amanda an article about it in *Life* magazine. The Beats thought practically everybody in America was too conformist, too much alike, and too interested in making money.

From the pictures in *Life,* it seemed that the Beats didn't wear shoes or comb their hair. For sure the girl

Beats did not use bobby pins or curlers at all. Amanda was amazed that Antoine, in France, would know about this when she, in America, didn't.

She told Margaret she had to write to her pen pal about it and she didn't know what to say. Margaret advised saying, "I don't dig the Beats."

Amanda adopted that sentence. She decided, since she was borrowing an idea from Margaret, it wouldn't hurt to pretend she *was* Margaret, just a little bit.

Lost Lake

December 29

Dear Antoine,

I hope your lip is fine, and I hope you have a very happy new year.

I am going out with friends for New Year's Eve. We hope we'll have a riot (ha-ha!). My father has made me promise not to drink and to be home by 12:30 a.m.

I have some personal questions. Do you circulate? Have you smelt Tender Fire? What do you think of it? Also, in your opinion, are the walking dead real?

(If you mind my asking these questions, you do not need to answer them.)

I don't dig the Beats. Why do you think they don't comb their hair or take baths? Do you think there is any meaning to this?

My best (girl) friend is a wonderful singer. Last week we snowshoed across Lost Lake and she sang beneath the spruces. It was very special, you would have liked it.

Sincerely,

Amanda K. Woods

P.S. Movies are pictures that move. Maybe the same as "cinema"? I have never had a bit of telephone. I do not know if I would like it.

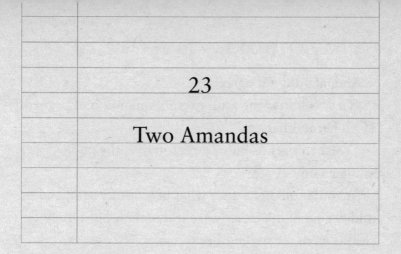

23

Two Amandas

School was grinding its way through February and spitting out the pieces like ice chips. Amanda was doing her arithmetic alone, on the corner table in the Loggers' Inn.

Pam was not coming to the hotel anymore to study. Amanda wanted her to, but she wouldn't. Her mother didn't want her to come, and she didn't want to, either.

The breakup had happened when Pam invited Amanda to stay over and Amanda's mother wouldn't let Amanda go. Her mother's reason was "we do not know the Collinses."

Amanda saw a problem in that right away, but her mother didn't.

"You two can be together. Pam can come here anytime, but you can't go to her house because we do not know her parents, and I am sure it is much nicer for her to come here than it would be for you to go there."

Amanda did not agree.

"Get to know the Collinses," Amanda had argued. "Call her mother up."

"You can't get to know a person over the phone," her mother said.

Amanda told her father what her mother said, and he told her he didn't exactly see it like that, but family decisions were for her mother to make.

In the privacy of Room 17, Amanda told Pam she couldn't come to sleep over, and why. Amanda could see that Pam was very upset, even though she didn't say so.

The next day after school, Pam told Amanda, "My mother says your mother thinks we're not good enough for your folks. We don't have a hotel. We don't belong to the Elks Club."

Pam said it in a snotty tone. Amanda never thought Pam could be like that.

"I want to stay over at your house!" Amanda said. "I am dying to come! I want to spend time with Max and Markie. I like your mom. I can't help it if mine won't let me go."

Pam said, "My mother won't let me go to the hotel anymore. She says I've been imposing on your father.

"We're still friends, though. Of course," Pam added.

Of course they were still friends, but they weren't really. They weren't mad at each other, but they weren't close the same way, either.

Amanda realized that for Pam she had stopped being Amanda and had turned into a representative of the Woods family. Pam had to be a representative of the Collins family, which was a proud and fine family of Rome, Wisconsin, in its own right, and Pam had to let the Woodses know that.

Amanda and Pam had both stopped being people and had turned into representatives. That was the way it was.

Amanda still was friends with everybody in the fifth-grade group. And Sheri Anderson, seeing that Amanda wasn't so close with Pam, invited Amanda to go skating one Saturday.

So they went, and Sheri was nice, but it wasn't like being with Pam.

She told her father that, trying to talk to him, the way Pam had suggested. He listened.

He said, "Well, of course, you don't know Sheri very well yet," and "It's good to get to know more than one person well, Amanda," and, finally, when what he said hadn't changed Amanda's sad face, he added, "Suffering is good for the soul." Amanda hated him.

All that was why Amanda wasn't in Room 17, which she felt unhappy being in without Pam, but back doing her arithmetic alone on a table in the dining room of the Rome Hotel, and it didn't matter at all, she thought, if she got the arithmetic right because she didn't want Room 17 anyway.

And yet in a way she wasn't alone. Right at the table in the Loggers' Inn, a fight had developed between Amanda Woods and Amanda K. Woods, and Amanda K. Woods was winning.

Amanda Woods did not give a piffle about anything. Amanda K. Woods wanted to get all 100s on her arithmetic, no matter what. Because Amanda K. Woods was a person, who, if she could possibly get something right, did get it right, a person who knew that quitting would never be her way.

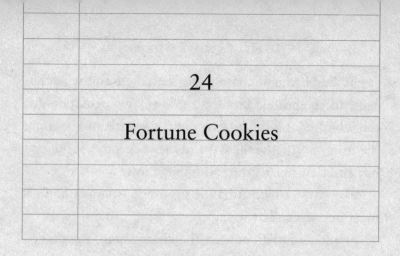

24

Fortune Cookies

In the second week of March, Margaret got accepted to Stanford, Swarthmore, the University of Connecticut, and Wellesley, the school she really wanted to go to. All the letters came in one week, but the Wellesley letter came last, saying Wellesley was "delighted" to welcome her to be part of the Class of 1959. When Margaret opened the letter and showed it to her mother, she clutched Margaret in her arms. "You did it!" she said.

To celebrate, the family went out to dinner at a new Chinese restaurant in Rome, the only one.

Amanda's mother left a whole plate of cold fried chicken in the refrigerator, though, just in case it turned out to be as people said, which was that Chinese food was good and filled you up, but you were hungry an hour later.

Her dad brought champagne with them to the restaurant, to celebrate Margaret's good news. Amanda got the job of taking the little wire off the cork and opening the frosty bottle. As she worked the cork loose, it popped out and flew across the room like a toy.

"Hooray!" called Amanda's mother. Amanda had almost never seen her so happy.

Amanda's father poured the champagne, some even for Amanda, and then each of them made a toast to Margaret.

They got three big platters of food to share, and little steaming bowls of rice. As they were starting to eat, their nearest neighbors at Lost Lake came in—the Moss family, who lived on the farm where the dirt road to Lost Lake left the highway.

They always saw the Moss family at church, but they didn't know them very well. Roger, the Mosses' only son, was a senior at Rome High, too.

Everybody said hello, and the Woods family shared champagne and toasted the Moss family. When their menus came, Amanda's dad told Mr. Moss which dishes had the most beef, because he figured Mr. Moss would want to know that, too, and then they got into a talk about farm prices, while Amanda's mother told Mrs. Moss that Margaret had just been admitted to four colleges, three in the East and one in California, and that was why they were celebrating.

"Congratulations, Margaret!" Mrs. Moss said.

"Margaret will be going back East," Amanda's mother said. "To Wellesley College."

Amanda knew the East was where the most culture was, but apparently Mrs. Moss either didn't or didn't care. "If I were seventeen and going to college, I'd choose California," she said. "It's so beautiful."

"Roger wanted to go away to school, too, but his father needs him on the farm. So he's going to take some courses on weekends down at Eau Claire State in the fall."

After dinner, the grownups ordered Chinese tea, and Roger asked Amanda and Margaret if they wanted to play pinball in the next room.

Pinball was Amanda's favorite game. She didn't think Margaret had ever liked it much, but this night she seemed to.

Roger Moss had brown hair with a wave in it, and an open face. There was quiet and softness in it that somehow reminded Amanda of Lost Lake when it was calm. His face didn't look all boarded up, like Margaret's old boyfriend Bob Bostwick's face. Roger congratulated Amanda on good plays—but he didn't put his hand on her head or call her "Champ."

Pinball was like life, Amanda thought, full of traps where you—the good little silver ball—could go down and never come up again—but also all kinds of ways you could slam yourself back into the game.

If you pulled a handle quickly enough to slam the levers, they hit the little silver ball and rescued it. Then the game, instead of ending, went on and on, while points flashed for you and bells went off, so it was really good, so that even though you knew that in the end all your little silver balls were going to drop through the holes of the pinball board into nothingness, never to be rescued again, you still triumphed.

Amanda had lost her best friend, but maybe in real life she could also get herself back into the game.

After they ran out of dimes, they went back and sat down with their families. The waitress brought everybody a thin crisp folded cookie, with a tiny slip of paper sticking out of the inside.

"Your fortune cookies," she said. Amanda didn't know what a fortune cookie was.

She picked up her cookie and looked into it. When had the paper gone inside? Before the cookies were baked, or after?

"You take the fortune out and read it," her father said. "After that you eat the cookie."

Everybody gently pulled their fortunes loose from the cookies, unfolded them, and read them out loud.

Her father said, " 'A clear mind does not fear evil.' "

Margaret said, " 'Quick! Smell the cherry trees in blossom.' But there aren't any around here," she added.

Her mother said, " 'One who lives in fear of thieves has already been robbed.' " She made the pursed-up disapproving face she always made when something she read was either very obvious or she didn't agree with it.

Roger Moss read, " 'Not every fruit is sweet.' "

Mr. Moss read, " 'Here is always the best place on Earth.' "

Mrs. Moss said, " 'If you want a garden, plant it.' Perfect! I just started tomato plants and herbs and petunias today. I just hope it doesn't turn too cold, even for the little greenhouse Bill fixed."

Amanda's fortune had been stuck in the cookie but then finally come out, even though it got torn in the process. She unfolded it and read, " 'You will be rich: wise laughter will be your golden treasure.' "

"Ah, money!" Mr. Moss said. "Amanda's lucky!" and everyone laughed, and then they pushed their chairs back and got up to go. Everybody left their fortunes behind on the tables except Amanda. She put hers in her pocket to take home, just in case it might be true, and because she didn't really understand it.

What was wise laughter? How did you know when you had it, and how old did you have to be before you got it, and did it make you rich in dollars, or was laughter itself the riches?

On the way home she asked where the fortunes came

from, and her mother said that the fortunes probably came from a Chinese fortune cookie factory in Chicago, where they worked hard to say things that couldn't mean very much, because they had to apply to everybody.

Amanda didn't argue, but she thought that even if the fortunes came from a factory, they could still be true and even inspired. At church, Father Bauer said God used all kinds of means to send people messages and keep them in touch with Him. God was sending messages all the time, Amanda figured. He could use clouds or trees or books or even a Chinese fortune cookie factory to say things if He wanted. And nobody, not even Amanda's mother, could be really sure He didn't.

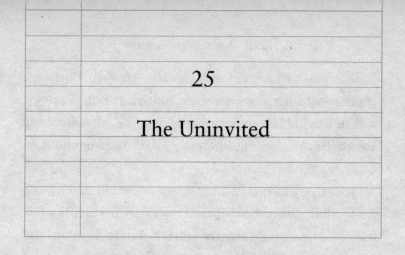

25

The Uninvited

Roger Moss had invited Margaret on a date—to a movie, *Come Back, Little Sheba*. Amanda wanted to go along. She had heard it was a movie about a dog.

She knew Margaret wouldn't invite her, but she hoped her mother would force Margaret to take her.

But even though Sheba was a dog, the movie was for adults, Amanda's mother said, and Amanda couldn't go. Amanda pointed out that the *Adventures of Robinson Crusoe* was also showing down the street in Rome, and it *was* a kids' movie, and she practically never saw movies. It would be easy for Roger and Margaret to drop her off at the other movie theater in Rome and pick her up afterward.

Her mother told her she had not been invited in *any* shape or form, it was rude to ask to go where you hadn't been invited, and she couldn't even ride along.

Amanda had never cared at all that Bob Bostwick never invited her anywhere: just to look at Bob Bostwick was to be glad not to be going along. She felt differently about Roger. They had played pinball together, and he was her friend.

He arrived to pick Margaret up in an old green Ford convertible. When he had visited with their parents a few minutes, he and Margaret started out to his car, and Amanda walked with them. She asked if Roger would like to see her horse.

"Sure," Roger said. Amanda called Skipper. He came to the fence and stretched his neck over it, hoping for a treat.

Roger walked over to Skipper and patted him.

"He's a beautiful pony," Roger said. "You're keeping him up really well."

"I curry him every day," Amanda said. She wanted to tell him more about Skipper, but she could see Margaret's eyes shooting poisoned arrows.

"If we don't go, we'll be late," Margaret said to Roger, sweetly.

"Right," Roger said.

He ran to open the car door for her, and Margaret smiled. Bob Bostwick, Amanda knew, had opened the car door for Margaret only a few times, when Margaret asked him to. And that one other time, when his car was in the Red Cedar River. Amanda thought of mentioning how polite Roger was, compared to Bob Bostwick.

She opened her mouth. Margaret's eyes were like cannons. The car door closed.

"Good night!" Amanda said.

Margaret didn't answer her.

Roger walked around to the driver's side of the car.

"Good night, Amanda," he said. "Hold down the fort." He backed the car out of the driveway to the road, and he and Margaret drove away. They didn't once look back.

All of a sudden Amanda felt she had lost not only them but her home and everything magic about it, including Skipper. Skipper was not a best friend, he was just a horse. Lost Lake was just a bunch of water. Where Amanda really lived was in the middle of nowhere, where it had been a miracle that just once she could get a friend to visit, and now that was all over.

Amanda ducked under the fence. In Skipper's pasture, she threw her arms around his neck and cried.

She heard footsteps on the gravel of the drive. "Amanda? A game of chess, Amanda?"

It was her father, looking for her.

Amanda didn't answer. She hid behind Skipper, but her father saw her. He, too, ducked under the fence.

"Amanda?" he said. "I thought we were going to play chess."

"I don't want to," Amanda said.

"Amanda—" her dad said.

"I don't want to!"

"Or we could fish—"

"I don't want to!"

"Amanda, it's not so bad."

"It is *terrible*!" Amanda said.

"Do you want to be alone?"

"I *am* alone!" Amanda said.

Her father turned away. Amanda grabbed his hand.

"Talk to me!" Amanda said. "Talk to me! You *never* talk to me! Nobody *ever* talks to me! And suffering is *not* good for the soul! That's a lie!"

Amanda squeezed her father's fingers and glared at him. He stood, letting her twist his fingers, but saying nothing. Amanda, through her anger, saw the sadness in his face.

"Maybe suffering isn't good for the soul, but it is life," he said. He talked almost hoarsely, like a person not used to talking, as if he hadn't heard his own voice for years.

"Mostly everybody is alone. We're just lucky when we're not. Margaret and Roger—they also probably feel alone most of the time. Now, tonight, they're just hoping they'll make one world out of two and not be alone.

"They don't know if they can do it. That's why they need to be alone together—to find out."

Amanda sniffled noisily. She wished she had a Kleenex.

Her father reached into his pocket. He held out his handkerchief.

"Someone is going to want to be with you, too, Amanda," her father said. "Someone is going to see you, and hope to make one world with you. When you're older, it will happen to you. It will.

"Amanda—you're going to be a teenager. The hardest part is waiting. Waiting and waiting for someone to see you in a special way. The only way to get through it is to have faith that it will happen."

Her father pulled his fingers free and held hers. "In the meantime, be like Mrs. Moss. Plant a garden."

Amanda pulled away. "That's so *stupid*! I can't make a garden here! Nobody can make a garden here. There's too much shade!"

"I'm talking about a garden inside you."

"There's no garden inside me! There's desert inside me!" Amanda said furiously.

"There's a garden, too," her father said.

Amanda did not turn her head. Amanda's father touched her hair. His hand felt heavy and strange. They hardly ever touched.

"There's a garden inside you already, Amanda," her father said. "I can't see it now, but I have seen it."

Amanda heard her father go back in the house, and her mother's voice asking, "Where's Amanda?"

"Taking care of Skipper."

Amanda stayed with Skipper for a long time. She got the curry comb from his tack room and curried him, even though it was dark and she couldn't see where she was brushing. She braided his mane very messily, just so she could unbraid it and brush it out again. She scratched him behind the ears. She filled her hands with oats, feeling his warm nose and his warmer breath in her palms, and then his big warm tongue licking up every last one. She started to feel real again—a little bit alive inside herself.

26

Persuasion

Saturday morning Amanda woke up feeling weak and light, but clear, like a person who has come through an illness.

Margaret was still sleeping with a peaceful smile on her face. Amanda said good morning to her mother, who was picking up the living room, and went on outside, looking for her dad. It was a warm day for April. He was down on the beach, looking at pieces of the dock and the diving board he had piled up there, ready to be set out in the water again.

"Good morning, little one!" he said.

"Can we talk more?" Amanda asked.

"All right," he said. "Let's go for a walk."

They walked along the shore of the lake, their feet crunching over gravel and thin patches of snow. They sat down on some rocks in the sun.

The ice on the lake was breaking up. Amanda looked across bobbing gray chunks of it toward the island.

"I had a friend," she said. "It was so hard, but I worked and I got a friend. I want my friend back! I want Pam to study with me again, but she'll never do it unless you help me."

"What do you want me to do?" her father said.

"You said Pam could study with me, but her mom thinks you don't like her. If you talk to Pam's mother, you can tell her that you like Pam, so she'll really know it."

Her father's face looked as board-like as Bob Bostwick's.

"I can't do that."

"Why not?" Amanda said.

"Young lady, I am your father and I don't have to give you reasons!" her father said.

"You are my father and you *ought* to give me reasons! You said you would talk to me and you aren't!"

Her father said nothing.

"I do not have one single friend in the world!" Amanda said.

Her father shifted his feet. Pebbles skittered across the old snow.

"The reason . . ." he began. He ground more pebbles under his boot heel. "It would be very, very embarrassing for me."

They parked in front of Pam's house. In the yard Max and Markie were building a snowman with bits of unmelted April snow. They ran up to Amanda and her dad.

"Look at this! Look at its nose!" they said. The snowman was small, because they didn't have much snow to work with, but they were pushing a big carrot into its face, and they had two apples for his eyes.

"It's a great face!" Amanda said. You couldn't actually say it was a great snowman, but a great face it was.

You should tell little kids what they did was great whenever you could, she knew. It was something she had learned from Pam.

They went up to the house and Amanda knocked. Her father had called ahead, so they knew Pam wasn't there, she was at her music lesson, but Amanda thought that didn't matter, it was better to talk to just Mrs. Collins. For her dad, two people could be more of an embarrassment.

Mrs. Collins opened the door and invited them in. She asked them to sit down in the living room, and then she offered Amanda's father coffee, but he said no, they were just going to stay a minute, and then he sat, turning the brim of his fancy city hat around and around in his hands. Mrs. Collins looked at him, but she didn't say a word.

"I just want to say," Amanda's father said, "that, uh, I'm very sorry something has come between Pam and Amanda. I think Pam is a marvelous girl. She is a wonderful friend for Amanda, and—you see, if it were up to me, Amanda would be here in a minute, as often as you would care to have her. She could learn so much from your family.

"It's just that Amanda's mother doesn't see it that way, and she is the one that makes the decisions about the children. She—I don't know why really. Some of her decisions would not be my decisions. But all families are like that, and she is the one that generally makes the home decisions, and I don't—haven't."

Mrs. Collins's posture had softened, but her face had not changed.

"But anyhow, the way things are is a tremendous loss to Amanda, and I feel that, I know that, and seeing our girls' happiness has been a great pleasure to me, too. We live out so far. Amanda has been very lonely at times, I think.

"I'd like to invite you and your husband, if he's home, to come by the hotel one afternoon, and bring your boys, too. We've got a very good banana cream pie, and we could all have a visit. I would like Pam to feel comfortable with us again. Amanda wants to be with her. I miss her, too."

"Whatever Pam wants," Mrs. Collins said. "I guess however things are, they are different from the way I thought."

The next week all the Collinses but Pam's dad came to the hotel, and everybody had Charley's banana cream pie. It might have been awkward, though, except for Max and Markie's excitement. The twins ran around looking at all the stuff in the Loggers' Inn and kept running back to the table to say what they'd seen. They wanted to know if they could come again.

Amanda's dad said that whenever Pam wanted to invite them, he would be happy to have them.

Pam said to her mother, "Do you want to see the room?" and everybody went upstairs.

Her dad unlocked the door to Room 17, and Mrs. Collins peered in.

"It looks like a good place to study—and to dream," she said.

"It is," Pam said, "it really is," and then Amanda knew everything was truly going to be all right.

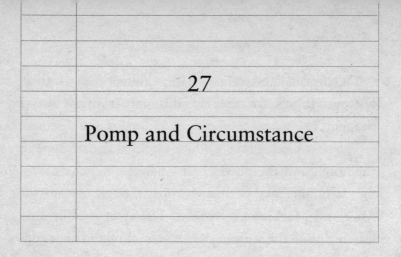

27

Pomp and Circumstance

Fifth grade turned out to be the best year in school that Amanda had ever had. The class made a theater and they put on plays about things that happened in families. Other kids liked the funny ideas that Amanda invented for the plays.

In science, they planted bean plants in tin cans and shined different-colored lights on them and then measured the plants to see which color light grew plants the fastest. For social studies, they visited the Rome newspaper office and got to see the very first issues of the Rome paper. As she looked at them, Amanda had almost felt that she was touching another time.

At the end of the year, her father invited the whole class to the hotel for ice cream, and explained to everyone lots about the history of Wisconsin and the photos on the wall.

Everybody liked Amanda's dad. Afterward, Mary Jane Stoltenberg thanked Amanda personally for getting her dad to invite them all to the hotel. Bob Larson wanted to know if Amanda got to go into the hotel and order ice cream free any time she wanted. Amanda said she could, and she didn't mind when everybody died of envy.

When spring came, sometimes instead of going to the hotel, she and Pam went to Pam's house and other girls' houses after school. Some Saturdays Amanda came into town with her dad and went roller-skating with Pam.

For the first time in years, the Rome Hotel was filled for June, so Amanda and Pam had to take their things out of Room 17. Her father said that when fall came and the number of travelers went down, they could use the room again—as long as Amanda kept getting 100s on her arithmetic.

For the first time ever, Amanda was sad about the prospect of school letting out. On the last day, Miss Deverest came into their room, not showing any traces of werewolf, and looking as if she had taken a few smiles from Miss Harmon's supply.

Miss Deverest told the class that Miss Harmon wanted to keep working with them and would be their sixth-grade teacher in the fall. Amanda was overjoyed.

After Miss Deverest left, Miss Harmon had little private conversations with each student. She told Amanda that she had shown the most improvement of anybody.

When she handed Amanda her report card, Miss Harmon gave her a hug and a kiss and said she was proud of her.

Outside, Amanda and Pam opened their report cards together. Pam had straight A's. Amanda had got straight A's except for a B in music and an A+ in arithmetic. When she showed it to her father, he said, "Good work, little one."

When they got home, her mother couldn't believe Amanda's grades or Miss Harmon's note on the report card that "Amanda has been an exceptional student and is a delight to know."

"Your teacher took a liking to you," Amanda's mother said, sounding as if she knew everything about it down to the last detail and had arranged it all herself. Somehow she made it sound as if Amanda had no part in her own success.

"I worked," Amanda said. "It isn't just that she liked me, I worked."

Her mother smiled, half-fondly, half-knowingly, and started to put Amanda's report card into her study desk where she kept all the others.

Amanda held out her hand. "I want it," she said. "It's mine and I want to keep it."

Her mother handed the report card to her. Amanda took it into her and Margaret's room and put it in the side pocket of her five-year diary. Then she dusted the diary.

The next day Amanda overheard her mother talking on the phone to someone, and saying, "Amanda is turning out to be a very good student. Outstanding at arithmetic . . . Which is the strangest thing."

Margaret graduated as valedictorian of the Class of 1955, and led the graduation procession. Gary Walber, the editor of the paper, walked with her up the aisle of the gymnasium of Rome High. He was salutatorian, but he looked happy—not as if his poor vulnerable ego was crushed by being second to a girl.

For a change, Margaret really looked like her photograph, with the "I am beautiful and I am going to be a doctor" expression on her face.

The music, "Pomp and Circumstance," sounded sad and stately. Hearing it, Amanda realized for the first time that one day, not too far off, Margaret would be leaving home.

After the ceremony, though, the summer of '55 seemed not so much different from any summer. Margaret went back to work at the hospital. Amanda came into town with her dad some days even though it wasn't school time. She saw Pam and they took the twins for picnics in the park.

One day Pam told her good news: in August, her family was going to spend a month canoeing, paddling north on lake after lake into Minnesota and all the way to Canada. They were going to see a lot. Besides that, Pam would have a good chance to get to know her father.

"I wish you could go with us," Pam said.

"I would love to go!" Amanda said.

But they both knew, without asking, that she wouldn't be allowed.

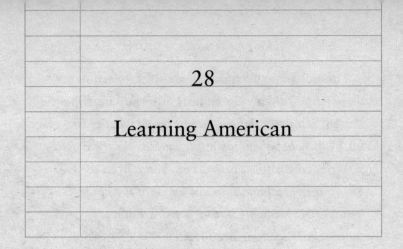

28

Learning American

Lyon
1 May

Dear Amanda,

You didn't answer my last letter. Maybe it was lost in postal strike. (Probably if you heard speak of riot, you also heard of this.) I will tell again what was in that letter.

Excuse me that I don't understand everything you write. I see that you kindly work very hard for to write very simple English for me, but still I don't understand it.

In school I am very good in English, I don't understand why I don't understand your English. My father says maybe it is the American that I don't understand.

[137]

I do not know what is "circulate." I looked in my dictionary, still I do not know. I hope I do it, if you think it is a good thing. I do not know what is "ha-ha," I only hope you were safe on New Year's Eve riot.

We have not smelt often. They come from the North Sea (Osmeridae) and I do not know of the kind Tender-fire. Probably it, too, is fishy. I don't understand "walking dead real."

My dictionary is English, not American. Maybe it is no good for American?

I do not understand "dig." In my English class we had a lesson called "Around Home" where I learned: "digging beets in the garden"; but I don't understand "digging the Beats." I believe generation Beats should comb the hair and bath themselves. In France, the philosophers bath themselves just like everyone else, maybe more. (In case maybe you thought that when I become one I shall not do it!)

Although I don't understand much of your letter, I have good news! Right now my family, we are packing for California. I am going to study American there during two months. In August we will tour the United States. I have shown your letters to my parents. They don't understand, either, but they think you must be very interesting. They want to meet you.

We will be in your Lost Lake in August. That will be

even better than a hit of telephone. I will be so happy to forget dictionaries and see your beautiful face!

   Sincerely,

   Antoine

                                        Lost Lake
                                        June 2

Dear Antoine,

   Do not come to Wisconsin. Minnesota is much safer and just as nice. Wisconsin can be very dangerous. The roads are bad. There are bears. Lost Lake is very lost. You could never find it without a guide, and there are no guides and nobody speaks French. People are not used to strange languages and I do not know how they will react.

   If you ever did find Lost Lake, you would be disappointed. You may not think so, but believe me, you would be.

   Please, for your own sake, don't try!

   Let's keep writing to each other!

   Very, very very sorry.

   Sincerely,

   Amanda

29

Raspberry Pie

In July, Roger's mother invited Margaret to a Sunday noon dinner at the Mosses' house. She went right after morning church.

Amanda was in bed reading when Margaret returned, kicking off her shoes and flopping down on their bed with a sigh. Her whole back landed on Amanda's side, where Margaret had no right to put it, and Amanda wanted to point that out, but she couldn't. There was a strange shimmering atmosphere around her sister like fireflies dancing that kept Amanda from opening her mouth.

"They are *nice*, you know that? *Really* nice!"

"Roger's folks?" Amanda said.

"Right! Roger's folks. They just make you feel so good! And he does, too."

Margaret was silent for a minute, and Amanda didn't say anything.

"They're not like us," Margaret confided, as if she was telling an enormous secret.

"What do you mean?" Amanda asked. She stretched out her legs a little but was careful not to hit Margaret in the side.

"They're just so nice," Margaret said. She smiled. "They're like—raspberry pie.

"We had the best dinner—chicken and dumplings with gravy, and fresh green beans from their garden, and raspberry pie. But the main thing is, when they talk to you, you don't feel like they're comparing you with everyone else they've ever met. They don't ask what your plans are. You don't have to say, 'Oh, Mr. Moss, I am a very serious person, my plan is this, my plan is that.' We talked about birds a lot—which ones they see around.

"And she—I mean, Mrs. Moss—made a really great pie. But she doesn't serve it like Mother. She didn't have a silver pie cutter and a Great Pie Announcement. The last time Mother made raspberry pie, don't you remember the Great Pie Announcement?"

Amanda didn't.

Margaret sat up, as if she were holding the silver pie cutter in her hand. "This raspberry pie is from a *French* recipe, and I *hope* you are able to appreciate it, and if you don't try it, George, I will be very upset, but don't take too big a piece because it's *very* rich, and you know you've been putting on weight lately, and you, too, Margaret, you need to be careful."

Amanda tried to remember the Great Pie Announcement. The last time her mother had made a raspberry pie, it was with wild raspberries that Amanda had picked. What she remembered was sitting at the table thinking, "Wild berries are the best. A million times better than tame berries, I picked these berries, that's why this pie is so good." Maybe when the Great Pie Announcement came, she hadn't been listening.

"Anyhow," Margaret continued, "Mrs. Moss brought out her pie all golden and rounded up over the pie plate with little bits of juice that had bubbled out on the crust, and she didn't say, 'This is *raspberry* pie,' because any fool could smell that it was raspberry pie, she just said, 'Margaret, would you like some pie?' and served me and then Roger and Mr. Moss and herself the size piece everybody wanted, but the thing is you could tell that if you said you didn't want any at all, that would be fine, and if you wanted three pieces, that would be fine, and if you even said you *hated* raspberry pie, that would be fine, too, because . . . because life is *big*!"

Amanda felt uncomfortable. "Mother's pie is good, too," she said.

"Yes, it is, but really the Mosses are great! You know what? They are better people than we are, even if they never heard of Wellesley, and even if they don't serve the water in stemmed glasses on Sunday, and even if they have farmer tans that end at their shirtsleeves. Except for Roger. *He* doesn't have a farmer tan," Margaret added, and then she blushed.

"Better people?" Amanda was feeling very upset.

"Maybe not better. Maybe just—happier."

"The thing is, our mother is really like the Lone Ranger."

"Our mother? Like the Lone Ranger?" Amanda was astounded.

"Yes. She's concerned about the world all the time. She wants to gallop in and rescue people, but she doesn't want to stay around them. She doesn't really like people, she just wants to save them."

Was it true? If you wanted to save people, didn't that mean you cared about them? It was just that their mother wanted people to be a certain right way, like the people who were supposed to build houses on Lost Lake and appreciate beauty, but never came.

"Mother likes a certain kind of people a lot!" Amanda protested.

"But there aren't many of them," Margaret said. "I'm not sure there really are *any*. For her. But for me"—Margaret smiled—"*he* is just like raspberry pie!"

Amanda couldn't follow Margaret's crazy mind at all.

"The Lone Ranger?" Amanda asked.

"*No!*" Margaret said, glaring at her. "*Roger* is just pure raspberry pie!"

She glared at Amanda for a minute more, and then she smiled.

"Anyway," she said, "I got a piece for you if you want it. It's in the bag on the chair. It got kind of mushed up— but I brought you a plate and a spoon."

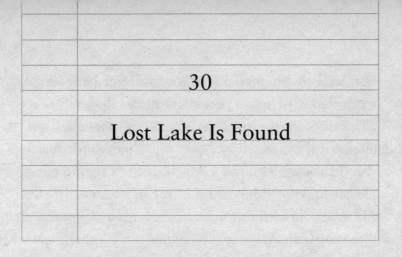

30

Lost Lake Is Found

Margaret painted the final "s" on a small sign she had made for the entrance to their driveway. The sign had four trees on it, two big sheltering ones that were supposed to represent their parents and two smaller ones that were supposed to be Margaret and Amanda. Underneath them Margaret had written in neat green letters: "The Woods."

She looked at her work with satisfaction. Then she took her paint can over to the north side of the house, got the ladder, and started painting a window frame bright green.

Amanda was working, too. She was in Skipper's pasture, currying him and hugging him. She had found a nice strip of loose, curling birch bark and put it on top of her head. Could birch bark ever make beautiful, practical hats, she wondered. The way the birch bark curled, it clamped hard onto a person's head and stayed there really well. Skipper seemed very interested in it until his attention was distracted by a car turning into the driveway.

A man, a woman, and a boy Margaret's age got out of the car, looking around curiously. Even from a distance, Amanda could tell they weren't from around Rome. All three had a special way of walking, a walk that almost had a smile in it, that said they knew they were strangers but felt at home anywhere.

Margaret studied the strangers from her ladder, looking highly displeased. She had a streak of green paint on her nose. Her naturally straight hair was in bobby pins so it would be curly in the evening when she went out with Roger. It was a fact of life that a girl had to look horrible in order to look really good later, but strangers had no right to come by unexpectedly and see you that way.

Amanda figured it was up to her to help the strangers. No matter how comfortable they looked, they had to be lost. She ducked under Skipper's fence and stepped onto the lawn.

The man pointed at Margaret's sign. It looked as if he was going to touch it.

"Wet paint!" Amanda shouted.

The woman took the man's arm and pulled his hand

away from the sign. The boy, ignoring them both, walked up the driveway.

As he got close, Amanda recognized him. He was not lost. He was the one person in the world Amanda would rather die than meet.

Antoine Bonnier halted at the foot of Margaret's ladder and gazed upward, beaming.

"Amanda!" he said. "In any place I would know you!"

"I'm not Amanda," Margaret responded crossly. "*She's* Amanda!" With her paintbrush, she pointed in Amanda's direction.

Amanda ran, ducking back into Skipper's pasture, stumbling past bushes and trees till she got to the lake. No one followed her. She stood panting, looking out over the water. Blue waves in rows, not knowing any better, marched fearlessly onto the sand.

If she didn't go back for a long time, Antoine might leave. Then Amanda would never have to face him. But then she would never know him either. Also, it was not nice to write to someone and trick him and pretend to be friends, and then, when he showed up, not even speak to him. That was not something Amanda K. Woods would do.

Amanda walked up the stone steps from the Woodses' beach toward their patio and the driveway. Red and yellow moss roses were growing out of the crevices at the edge of the steps, and Amanda paused to pick some, just as if it was what she had had in mind all along.

In the clump of people that was the Bonniers and Margaret, Antoine was the one who saw her first. He walked toward her, smiling.

She remembered her birch bark hat and was afraid she looked foolish. Quickly she tore it off her head and threw it onto the grass.

In a second they would meet. Amanda rubbed her Lyle Leveridge hand on her jeans. Abruptly she realized that she smelled very much like a horse. And Antoine liked to bathe! If only she had bathed! Or if she had put on lots of Tender Fire perfume! Even though he thought it was fishy, with enough of it on, a person might at least smell seventeen. But it was too late for that now. Antoine was at her side.

He sniffed. His mouth curled down, his eyebrows went up, and his eyes shone with laughter. "The air here is indeed wonderful," he said. He took Amanda's Lyle Leveridge hand and raised it high, as if it were delicate and beautiful.

"Miss Amanda K. Woods," he said. "Enchanted."

Amanda nodded. Something in her throat had grown into a strange numbness the size of a golf ball, and she couldn't speak. Gracefully she bowed. She handed Antoine the moss roses.

With a bow of his own, Antoine took the flowers and handed them to his mother.

"Flowers," he said, in a beautiful accent.

"Very pretty," Mrs. Bonnier said, in the same beautiful accent.

So she would smell better, Amanda pulled the curry comb out of her back pocket and threw it toward Skipper's pasture. Then she rubbed both her hands on her jeans and shook hands with Antoine's parents.

"Amanda, we so much enjoyed your fine and mysterious letters," Antoine's father said. "We have been curious to meet you."

Amanda nodded.

Margaret said, *"Un peu de l'eau?"*

Amanda heard, *"On poo duh low?"* She figured it must be French, because Mrs. Bonnier seemed to know just what it was and said something like, *"No, mare see."*

Another car rolled into the driveway—Amanda's father. The golf ball dissolved in Amanda's throat. She could speak!

"Here comes my father!" she said. "I'll introduce you."

He walked up to them all, with a cordial, inquiring gleam in his eyes. Her father was so at ease with strangers! Maybe more at ease with strangers than with people he knew. Amanda remembered how you were supposed to do introductions. She took a deep breath and got all the words out:

"Daddy, I would like to introduce you to Antoine, my pen pal from France, and his parents, Mr. and Mrs. Bonnier."

"Antoine, Mrs. Bonnier, Mr. Bonnier," her father said, "I'm very pleased to welcome you to Lost Lake, and to our home. My wife is off playing bridge, but when I tell her you're here I'm sure she'll be very eager to meet you."

Amanda hadn't expected her father to sound so warm and so comfortable! She admired his manners very much. They were almost—French.

"I sent you a letter," Amanda said, "telling you how much . . . trouble . . . it could be to get here."

"Antoine did receive your letter," Mrs. Bonnier said. "It seemed to us a challenge."

"You were so kind to worry," Mr. Bonnier said. "But we had no trouble to arrive. None at all."

Amanda's father invited everyone into the house. Amanda and Margaret started coffee brewing for everyone and then hurried back into their room. Amanda took a washcloth from the bathroom and quickly scrubbed herself. When Margaret's head was turned, she borrowed quite a bit of Tender Fire.

Margaret stopped pulling bobby pins out of her hair.

"Amanda," she said, "why did your pen pal think I was you?"

"It was an accident," Amanda said. Guilt blazed into her head: she had taken Margaret's photo; she had written: "Margaret, who is sometimes a pain in the neck, but I think she will grow up someday."

Margaret stared at her.

Amanda put her thumbs together below her chin. The fingers on her maybe average left hand clung desperately to the fingers on her Lyle Leveridge enchanting right hand.

"I mean, I tried to copy the way *you* sound when I wrote him, to sound older. And I knew about the Beats, because you told me what to say. So . . . he thought I was older. That's all."

Margaret dropped a bobby pin on her desk, and her suspicions seemed to drop with it. "Well, if I had known he was coming, I would have dressed up!" she said.

"Me too," Amanda said.

When, in fresh clothes, Amanda and Margaret brought coffee into the living room, it seemed everyone was settling in for a good long visit. The Bonniers were making plans to stay overnight at the Rome Hotel, and Amanda's father was inviting them to dinner there. He had phoned Amanda's mother right in the middle of her bridge game. She would come to dinner at the hotel, too.

Antoine looked at Margaret a lot. He told her he hoped she was coming to dinner.

When she said she was sorry but she had a date, he looked disappointed.

Still, he also looked at Amanda often, and every time he did, he was smiling. She decided she could smile, too—and then she realized there was something she wanted very much for him to see.

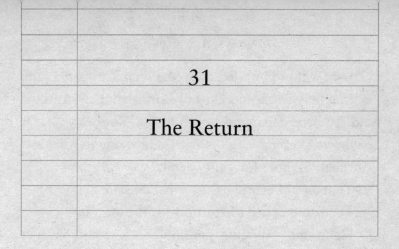

31

The Return

Amanda's dad said the two of them could ride Skipper double, as long as they didn't go too far. Amanda rode in front, with Antoine behind the saddle, straddling Skipper's bare back. Her dad came out to see them off.

"Don't make Skipper run. The two of you are quite a load," he said. "You're growing out of your horse, Amanda. It's soon time you got a big one."

"Skipper *is* a big horse!" Amanda said, and she and Antoine rode away.

"Did you hear that?" Amanda said to Antoine. "My dad might want me to give up Skipper. How could he?"

"Well, if you get too big," Antoine said.

"But I never want to get too big for Skipper!" Amanda said.

"Then just don't eat much," Antoine said. "Stay small."

"But I want to be taller than Margaret," Amanda said.

"Maybe you should eat tall skinny foods," Antoine said. "Celery, asparagus, green beans. Not beets . . . Or maybe you can have two horses, a new one to ride, and Monsieur Skipper for your friend."

"That would be the best!" Amanda said.

They had reached the turnoff for the meadow.

"Hang on!" Amanda said. She neck-reined Skipper and he clambered onto the ghost road.

"It's the end of it that's the most special part," she said. "In a little while we'll get there."

And it did seem just minutes till the road ended and they entered the meadow, its flowers shining in the sun.

"What a beautiful place!" Antoine said. "And it is so wild. The wildness here must come into people and make them beautiful, too. Maybe."

"Maybe," Amanda said.

"The flowers are like little suns," Antoine said.

"This place was here for years, but I never knew it," Amanda said.

They got down from Skipper and walked into the flowers.

"Antoine," Amanda said, "I just thought you wouldn't write to me if I sent you my own picture."

"I think I would have written to you anyway," Antoine said. "Your letters are very entertaining."

"Did I sound seventeen?" Amanda asked.

"The part I could understand, yes. For the rest—if I had a little sister, I would like it if she sounded like you."

"If I had a brother," Amanda said, "I wish he would be like you."

She looked toward Skipper. "Over there," she said, pointing, remembering, "last summer I found a four-leaf clover."

A year had passed since Amanda had seen the meadow. It had died under the snow and been reborn. It was still totally beautiful, she thought, unchanged except for one thing. It wasn't lonesome anymore.

32

Dear Diary

Antoine Bonnier is my friend! Even though I tricked him. He is wonderful! He says he wishes he had a sister like me. We went on a long ride and talked. I taught him words "in American." But he couldn't understand circulating, even when I explained it. He said if he felt like going out with friends, he did, and if he felt like staying home, he did that. I don't know what the word is for that, but it sounds like more fun than "circulating."

I will write much more later, because right now I feel so happy I can't sit still—I want to swim and dive and dive and dive. (Then I'll have to get ready fast for dinner with Antoine and his family.)

I feel like a rainbow.

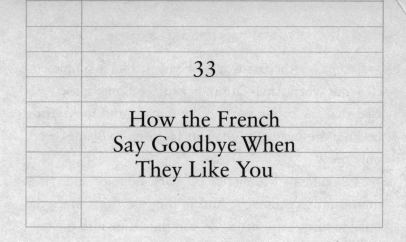

33

How the French
Say Goodbye When
They Like You

At dinner, there were candles on the table, and everyone sparkled and laughed and got along. Amanda's mother found out that her favorite French recipes were some of Mrs. Bonnier's favorites, too—which made it 100 percent sure that the recipes were really French. When Amanda's mother found out that both the Bonniers were professors of mathematics, she was very impressed. She told the Bonniers, "Amanda is very gifted—especially at math," and Mr. Bonnier said, "If you are interested in mathematics, I will show you something you should know."

He took a long strip of paper from his pocket, twisted it once, and brought the two ends together with one twist. He joined the ends with a bit of candle wax, and then he handed the strip to Amanda.

Except for the twist, it looked just like a simple circle—but when Amanda ran her finger along it, she realized that the inside became the outside and the outside became the inside, so that, in fact, the two sides were only one.

"It is called a Möbius strip," Mrs. Bonnier said. "It is important to geometry. And in life, too, sometimes the outside turns into the inside and the inside into the outside."

"Keep it," Mr. Bonnier said. "Let it be a souvenir of our visit! Of course, if this one gets ruined, anytime you can make many more."

The next morning Amanda went into town with her dad to have breakfast with the Bonniers and say goodbye to them. She would have asked Margaret, too, but Margaret was still sleeping, so she didn't wake her.

Charley cooked them a French breakfast, what he called crepes suzettes—thin pancakes that came to the table flaming. Then he sat down with the Bonniers and told them about the French traders who had explored Wisconsin, and about the old logging days.

Afterward, Amanda drove with the Bonniers around Rome and showed them things, the beautiful bandstand in the park, where there weren't concerts anymore because, instead of going to the park, people stayed inside and watched TV; the Red Cedar River; Pam's house, where, without Pam there, it was impossible to say what was so great about it; and their school, which looked blank and boring without children—that is, people— around it.

Then the Bonniers drove Amanda back to the hotel. They said goodbye to Amanda's father.

In the hotel lobby, Antoine took a red beret from his pocket and handed it to Amanda.

"For when you do not want to wear the tree bark," he said.

"Thank you!" Amanda said. She put it on.

"Not so," Antoine said. "Not straight." He set the beret farther back on Amanda's head at an angle. "Now you look French."

Amanda looked at herself in the lobby mirror, her cheeks flushed, her hair shining under the red beret.

Did she look French? Anyhow, she liked the way she looked.

She turned to Antoine. "But I don't have a gift for you!" she said.

"You give me the pleasure of knowing you," Antoine said. "That is the best gift."

"It's a pleasure to know you, too!" Amanda said. She hoped that Antoine would send more letters to her, but she didn't want to ask.

As if he'd read her thought, Antoine said, "I'll write." He bent down and whispered in her ear, "You can be my little sister." He hugged Amanda and kissed her quickly, once on each cheek.

Then Mr. and Mrs. Bonnier also each kissed Amanda once on each cheek. By the time she kissed Antoine's dad, Amanda realized that in France, as the other person kissed you on each of your cheeks, you were supposed to kiss him on each of his cheeks, and she actually managed to do it.

It must have taken the French centuries of civilization to figure out their double kiss, Amanda thought. Probably they couldn't even begin to work on it until they had given up the guillotine.

When she got back home, her mother wanted to know if she realized that the Bonniers were very special people and that being a mathematician was a very special thing, and that Amanda could be a mathematician one day, too, if she wanted.

And Amanda thought how wrong people could be when they thought about what you could or couldn't do, based on what you were already doing.

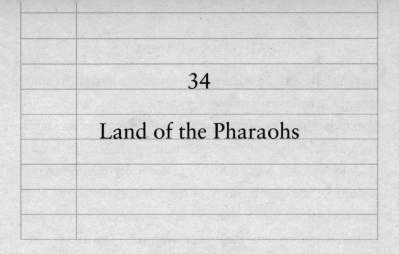

34

Land of the Pharaohs

The packing for Margaret's trip East to Wellesley took three days. Margaret had given up her job at the hospital to prepare for going away.

There wasn't enough space in Margaret and Amanda's room to pack, so Margaret and her mother had moved all the living room furniture to one side and set the two steamer trunks being used for the trip in front of the fireplace. In the evenings, Amanda's dad stayed out on the porch reading—to keep out of the way, he said.

He wasn't interested in the packing, but Amanda was fascinated. It reminded Amanda so much of what they'd studied in Miss Harmon's class about the burial of the Egyptian pharaohs.

What made it like the burial of the pharaohs, of course, wasn't that Margaret was dying or being buried but that everything she owned was going into the trunks, and the whole process was very serious. As it all went in, Amanda thought someone should have been swinging incense, as maybe ancient Egyptian priests did. It seemed as if everything was so well and carefully packed that it would be preserved, not just for a train trip to the East but for a thousand years.

In went five new cashmere sweaters, ten skirts, five Oxford-style blouses, and two pullover sweaters; one pair of jeans for the dorm, and one pair of slacks for the country; two girdles, one of which allowed breathing and another for occasions when you wanted to look really thin and breathing didn't matter; a hat for church, gray felt with a blue-green feather on it; three party dresses, two basic black and one red; white gloves for spring and summer parties, black suede gloves for winter; and real cultured pearls, a graduation present from Margaret's godparents.

All the clothes had to go in very carefully, with layers of tissue paper between them and within their folds, so that nothing would get crushed. The tissue paper was very important. When Margaret unpacked, her mother said, everything would look as if it came directly from a hanger in her closet, without a wrinkle. Underneath the clothes went layers of heavier stuff: three pairs of shoes, and two pairs of winter boots, one to really deal with snow and another pair for dates; Margaret's winter jacket and her winter coat; the pictures of all her friends from high school and her senior yearbook, which said she was the most popular girl in her class.

They called Amanda's dad off the porch for advice on packing the appliances: Margaret's radio–alarm clock; a brand-new electric popcorn popper in which you could also heat soup for all your friends, and which Amanda's mother was sure would make Margaret very popular; an electric coffeepot so she could make coffee when she was studying; her typewriter; her hair dryer, which looked like a typewriter until you opened it, and then a long hose and a big plastic helmet appeared, ready to go around the largest-size curlers and dry the wettest hair in thirty minutes, just as well as the giant hair-drying helmets at the beauty parlor; Margaret's slide rule; and her *Advanced Biology* book and Dale Carnegie's *How to Win Friends and Influence People*.

Amanda's dad advised them to protect all the appliances by packing them in towels and washcloths, so they did.

On the evening of the third day of packing, when they were just about to close the trunks, Margaret dug into her closet and brought out her old stuffed panda bear. He had no fur on his stomach because Margaret had carried him around so much, his button eyes were loose but hanging on, and his nose was completely smashed in. He looked surprised but pleased to be thought of after so many years, and, having survived kindergarten and grade school, suddenly to be going away to college.

Amanda's mother looked surprised at seeing the panda bear, but all she said was "Be careful that bear doesn't crush any clothes!"

After Amanda wrote in her diary about the packing and the pharaohs, she felt let down. But then she realized she could tell Pam about it when Pam got back from her vacation. And she could write Antoine about it. Now he knew her. Now when she wrote, she wouldn't have to pretend to be somebody else. She could say her own real thoughts, and he would understand.

35

A Future Is
Something You Protect

Amanda's mother had sent her out fishing. Probably her mother had thought Amanda would be gone for hours, but Amanda had caught a lot of fish quickly and come home to clean them.

She was standing in Skipper's pasture outside her parents' bedroom window, about to bury the fish heads and entrails, when the serious conversation about Margaret's future started.

Amanda was probably not supposed to hear any of it, but in fact she heard the whole thing.

Her mother and Margaret were in the bedroom, and her mother was looking for something more to give Margaret—three embroidered linen handkerchiefs with lace around the edges, which would be good to perfume and carry in an evening bag to the theater, her mother said.

"Because of course you will go to the theater. You couldn't live so near Boston and not go. Theater is part of the life of any civilized person."

"The handkerchiefs are pretty," Margaret said.

Amanda was going to stick the spade in to start burying the fish heads, but she stopped when her mother said, as if it had just occurred to her for the first time, "You do like Roger Moss very much, don't you, Margaret?"

"He's a nice person," Margaret said.

"And he likes you *very much*," Amanda's mother said, in that tone she had of knowing everything.

"He likes me some," Margaret said.

"You know, Margaret, this concerns me. I don't think you should leave Roger dangling."

"I'm not," Margaret said. Then she added, as if she couldn't help herself, "Roger is Roger: he's not 'dangling.' "

"Is he going to write to you?"

"Maybe," Margaret said. "If he wants to."

"What I am afraid is that he might be too serious about you. A boy like Roger is not right for you, Margaret."

"Maybe not," Margaret said.

"You have been having a summer romance—and summer romances end," Margaret's mother said.

"Sure. Of course," Margaret said. "Mother—I don't want to talk about this."

"Your not wanting to talk about Roger is just the reason we *should* talk, Margaret. It makes me worried that you're too serious about him."

"I am not 'too serious' about him!" Margaret said.

"Then certainly you're going to disappoint him," Margaret's mother said.

"I'm leaving. He knows I'm leaving!" Margaret said.

"These things can drag on and drag on. I would hate for Roger to think there's a future in waiting for you. I would hate for you to think there's a future with Roger."

"Who knows?" Margaret said. "How are you so sure you know?"

"I do know!" Margaret's mother said. "Roger Moss is the kind of boy who could *ruin* your life! The whole world is opening up for you, Margaret. If I had had your chance . . . I wouldn't have looked twice at Roger Moss! You're going to enter the best society, meet the most accomplished people. Roger Moss is *nothing* compared to the kind of people you're going to know."

"Roger is not nothing. How dare you say he's nothing!" Margaret cried.

"I didn't mean it that way! Of course he's not nothing, darling," Amanda's mother said soothingly. "The point is, the best way to go to a new life is to go unattached—

to go not looking back. Not diminishing your new life by hanging on to the old one."

"I am one person now and I am going to be the same person out East!" Margaret said.

"When you get there, maybe yes. But you're going to change, Margaret. You're going to change a lot."

"I suppose. I suppose everybody changes," Margaret said. "But that doesn't have anything to do with Roger."

"You know the changes are coming. Begin them now. You know you're going to want to date when you're out East."

"I suppose so. I haven't thought about it."

"You haven't talked about it with Roger?"

"No," Margaret said.

"Well, that isn't fair to Roger, is it? Or to you. You really must talk to him, Margaret. Let him know now that you need your freedom!

"You really must do it. Believe me, it will make everything easier for him, and for you, too. *Will* you do it?"

Margaret said nothing Amanda could hear, but maybe she had nodded her head.

"And then tell him we've decided that it's fine for him to come to your going-away party with all your other friends—but not to come to the station to say goodbye at the train. That's just for family."

"But I want him to come to the train!"

"Margaret—you don't want to give Roger the idea

that you're closer to him than you really are. I have great expectations for you. I always have. All your life, Daddy and I have helped you every way we can. We're giving you the finest education there is."

"I *earned* it! I could have it anyway. I could have a full scholarship to Wellesley or anywhere. I'm that good!" Margaret said.

"The thing is, dear, you never could have had a full scholarship. Daddy makes too much money. No school would give you one because our family income is too high. If it weren't for us—for Daddy—you wouldn't be going. Don't you think you owe us a little consideration? Can't you give a little attention to us? To your family? To how we think? To what we want?"

"This is what Daddy wants, too?" Margaret asked.

"Of course he agrees with me," Margaret's mother said.

"All right!" Margaret said. "*Now* can we talk about something else?"

And Margaret's mother said, of course.

In the middle of the night the bed moved, and Amanda woke up. Margaret was moving around in the dark, a flashlight in one hand and tissue paper in the other. She took the corsage of roses Roger had given her for the prom off the bulletin board and looked at it, and started to wrap it, but as soon as the tissue paper touched it, the corsage shattered and all the petals fell.

36

The Last Dance

Amanda was helping with Margaret's goodbye party. In the end there were only nineteen people, including Margaret. Roger Moss wasn't coming at all.

Amanda wanted to know why.

"Because he's not coming to the train because that's for family, so he's not coming to the party, either," Margaret said. "But it's for the best," she explained. "If he wants to be like that, he can just be like that! It's up to him. It's not my fault he doesn't understand anything. I'm not mad. He's the one that's mad!"

So the party was just Margaret's and Roger's friends from Margaret's graduating class—but not Roger.

Amanda and Margaret's mother and father greeted everybody as they arrived and shook their hands, but they stayed upstairs while Margaret and her friends had their party on the beach.

Some of the people at the party knew Roger and Margaret had broken up and some of them didn't. The ones that didn't asked, "Where's Roger?" and then others said, "Shush," which Margaret either didn't hear or pretended she didn't hear.

The party was a hot dog and marshmallow roast, with a fire down by the lake. Everybody was eighteen, so Amanda's mom and dad said since it was legal they could have beer, as long as they didn't have more than two each. Margaret had asked Amanda to play the music for the party, so she was part of it, too.

After a while the friends started laughing and talking about funny things that had happened in the four years they were in high school together, and the girls fed hot dogs and marshmallows to their boyfriends and vice versa. It was a cold night, like autumn already, so nobody swam, but Amanda plugged Margaret's hi-fi record player in downstairs after everybody ate, and she played all the records Margaret had stacked up and wanted played—the tiny 45 RPM records not much bigger than doughnuts that had only one hit song on a side. Amanda had to watch them all the time, because they were over before you knew it, and Margaret had said she didn't want any gaps in the music coming about because Amanda forgot what she was doing.

Amanda spun "Dance with Me, Henry," "Mister Sandman," and "Earth Angel." She played "Autumn

Leaves" and "Sh-Boom" and lots more. For a little while Margaret just watched while everybody danced, and kept busy picking up paper plates, but then her best girl-friend Sandra told her boyfriend Mike to dance with Margaret, and after that all the girls told their boyfriends to take a turn dancing with Margaret so she wouldn't feel alone.

Margaret had on a sleeveless pink dress with a flared skirt that fanned out as she danced. She had put on a lot of powder all over her face to keep it from looking red, and she laughed a lot, but sometimes her lips with her reddest lipstick on them looked as if they had been cut out of her face with scissors and her laugh sounded like tin cans falling from high up and landing on a concrete floor.

Amanda played "Rock Around the Clock." It was a brand-new kind of music called rock 'n' roll. Then she chose a slow song, "Cry Me a River."

Gary Holmes, who was Roger's best friend, asked Margaret to dance to it. As they danced past Amanda, she heard Gary whisper to Margaret, "I'm sorry," and then Margaret hugged him very hard and started to cry, and Amanda didn't know what to do when the record stopped because that was the last one, so she started playing them all over again.

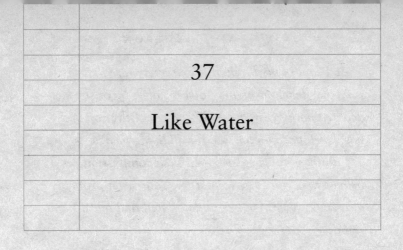

37

Like Water

The day of Margaret's departure, a letter arrived for Miss Amanda K. Woods. It was from India and had a stamp on it showing a man in a gorgeous robe riding an elephant. Vikram Savananda, the swami Amanda had written to so long ago about Bob Bostwick, had at last responded to her question.

> *Delhi, India*
> *June 21, 1955*

Dear Miss Woods,

I am sorry to say that my publisher has been slow in forwarding your letter, and so my response is delayed.

I am glad your sister was not hurt in the car spin. Many times we have premonitions of danger that can help us to avoid harm. However, I do not think you have developed higher powers.

As I said in my book, it is extremely rare that someone develops higher powers unless he or she has devoted many years to study and concentration and has developed compassion for all living beings.

I doubt you have developed such compassion yet. I believe that you envy your sister. Your sister probably also envies you. Ask her, and you will find out if I am right.

We need not be ashamed of envy. It is natural. However, when we devote our minds to understanding ourselves and others, our envy and fears fall away.

Since you wish to have higher powers, you may want to develop your compassion. How can you do this? I would advise you to be like water. Water is sensitive, but calm and clear. Even if water is beaten with a stick, the stick will leave no marks. Water can be disturbed by the wind, but when the wind goes it will return to its original nature. Water is soft, but it shapes the mountains and the earth. Water looks to the sky and is a mirror of the universe.

No matter who tries to block it, water seeks the path it must follow. No one can diminish it. It is always complete, and its home is everywhere.

My very best wishes, Miss Amanda K. Woods.

I salute God in you,

Vikram Savananda

Amanda looked at Margaret, who was clearing things out of her desk and putting them into a cardboard box. The box was going into storage in the basement temporarily. Before spring, a new room for Margaret would be built onto the house, and then the things she was leaving behind would go into it.

Margaret worked grimly. Ever since the party, all the closeness Amanda and Margaret had shared was gone. Margaret was back to treating Amanda like a mosquito, just like the old days.

Amanda wanted to talk to Margaret about the letter from Vikram Savananda, but it didn't seem like a good time. She wanted to ask Margaret if she envied her, but it didn't seem like a good time for that either. But maybe it was the only time that the question would ever make any sense.

Amanda quieted herself, and tried to feel like water. She said, "Margaret, have you ever envied me?" She thought Margaret would say "No and shut up," but maybe because Amanda had asked in a considering way, Margaret dropped a load of stuff into the box and sat up, and actually thought about it.

"Envy *you*?" Margaret repeated. "I don't think so."

"Are you sure?" Amanda persisted. And then Margaret exploded.

"I could never envy a persistent little gnat like you!

You are very conceited in your opinions. You are only twelve years old, but you always think you know what's right, and you think, just because an opinion is your opinion, it must be the truth. You don't know how to work at all, everybody has always spoiled you, you think currying a horse is a big important piece of work."

"I *have* worked!" Amanda protested. "I really do know what work is." She was thinking of the arithmetic, the endless horrible long-division problems she had conquered. But Margaret ignored what she said and just went on talking.

"Not like me. I was not dumb like you," Margaret said. "I knew nobody was going to like just plain me. Mother didn't even like just plain me. I worked to do well in school. I worked so people would like me. And Mother and Daddy let you get away with everything, and everybody says you're so sweet and charming, and you never worked at anything in your life! Even Roger—"

She stopped and did not continue.

"Roger what?" Amanda said.

"Thought you were cute," Margaret said. She dropped her head, concealing it in the drawer she was emptying.

"Maybe I envy your ignorance," Margaret said. Her voice sounded hollow, as if she were down at the bottom of a well.

Amanda tried to stay like water, absorbing into herself what Margaret had said without its hurting.

Margaret lifted her head from the drawer. "To give you credit," she said, "you are not as bad as you used to be." Then she sat on the floor with her back to Amanda, so Amanda couldn't see her face.

And Amanda felt bad for her, because she knew whatever was in the papers Margaret appeared to be looking at, she was really thinking about Roger Moss.

Amanda forgot the things Margaret had just said. In her heart she felt compassion like a sudden wound. She wanted to give something to Margaret, something for her going away, something that would be the best thing Amanda had.

"Margaret," she said.

Margaret looked up.

"Margaret, if you want, I'll give you the four-leaf clover—the one on the bed . . ."

Margaret looked up at the four-leaf clover in its little bed of white wax and glared at Amanda.

"That stupid thing!" she said. "I wish it would fall down!"

Amanda clenched her fists. "It hasn't fallen down for a year, and it will never fall down, and you are *stupid* not to care about luck!" Amanda shouted.

And it was as if for the first time she had used the

sharpness that flashed in the "K." in her name, and in herself. And she was proud, because she was finally standing up to Margaret, but then Margaret stood up with tears running down her face and walked quickly out of the room.

The bathroom door slammed shut.

Amanda looked at Swami Savananda's letter, which was a big mistake mostly because it had come at the wrong time. She knew he was right about one thing. She *had* envied Margaret in the long-ago past when she went out with Bob Bostwick, and earlier than that, and much more recently, too. However, at this particular moment, as she held the letter, she didn't.

Amanda realized that Swami Savananda was probably a Hindu and she wondered if it was all right for a Christian to try to be like water. Jesus hadn't tried to be like water, He had walked on it. But also He had been baptized in it, so He must have had some respect for it. And also He had said, "Blessed are the peacemakers."

Amanda got up, went to the bathroom door, and listened. There were no sounds from inside. She knocked with her Lyle Leveridge hand, but Margaret didn't say anything. She tried the doorknob. It was locked.

"Margaret," Amanda said, "I know you aren't stupid, and I'm sorry."

From the other side of the door there was no answer.

Amanda couldn't think of anything else to say.

How could you learn to be like water? Amanda did not know.

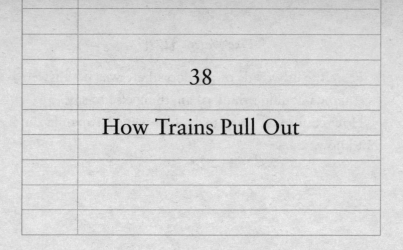

38

How Trains Pull Out

With scrapes and panting and quick united lifts, her dad, her mother, and Margaret got Margaret's two trunks and suitcase into the back of the station wagon. Then the Woods family went out to have a late dinner at the Elks Club to celebrate Margaret's going to college. Margaret was wearing clothes their mother thought would be comfortable for sitting up all night on the train: a red plaid skirt and a white long-sleeved blouse with a cameo pin. Margaret's eyes looked bleary, and her face was almost as red as her skirt.

They all had fish platters, and all they really talked about was the food, and a little bit about Beryl Chalmers from Long Island, who was going to be Margaret's roommate at Wellesley, and who for five years had played the harp in a regional orchestra. Amanda's father set out to give Margaret advice.

"Now, don't you worry about that harp," he said. "You have character and brains, and that girl will respect you."

"Musical people can be friendly," Amanda said.

Margaret looked as if she wished they'd stop talking, as if of course she wasn't worrying about Beryl Chalmers in the least.

Amanda's dad, who usually never said anything, just kept on.

"Don't worry over what-all she knows about music. You don't have to tell people all you don't know. Just listen and learn. People are going to like you, Margaret. They always have."

He started dabbing at his eyes with his napkin. And then he coughed and said, "Excuse me," and got up and left the table.

Their mother looked around the Elks Club to see who might be watching and seemed relieved when nobody was. She turned to Margaret.

"Do you know, Margaret, I just read that only 6 percent of all the doctors in the entire United States are women? You are going to be one of a very select group!"

Margaret said nothing.

"You have a great future, Margaret," her mother continued. "And even though you're going to a girls' school, you don't have to worry, there are going to be plenty of boys around you. In a month you'll be dating men from Harvard!"

Then just like her dad, Margaret got up and left the table, and despite all her years of training, she didn't even say "Excuse me."

Margaret and their dad came back after a while, sat down, and picked at their food. Then it was time to go. When they left the club, the bartender, the manager, and the waitress all congratulated Margaret and wished her the best, and for a minute Margaret smiled and looked almost happy. Rome, Wisconsin, knew and respected her.

There was nobody at the train station when they got there. Amanda got Margaret's suitcase. Amanda's father on one side and her mother and Margaret on the other hauled the steamer trunks out of the back of the car and wobbled and scraped them up next to the tracks, where the train crew would get them.

The waiting room was closed, so they stood outside. Sometimes the "400" train to Chicago could be late, that's what her father said—sometimes it was even a half hour late—and he looked at his watch. Then he said he thought they all ought to stand back a ways, because the train might smoke, and there was no use breathing that.

They stood about thirty feet back from the track and listened. Margaret must have been listening hardest, because she was the first to hear it: a thin fine whining sound along the rails that seemed to vibrate, thicken, and accelerate as it got closer, and then there was the wail of the whistle, and the train itself pulling up before them, with black cars and a yellow engine.

Seen so close, the "400" was huge. In the passenger cars, some people were asleep and some were reading magazines, never even looking out to see what they could of Rome, Wisconsin. Back two cars was a dining car. Amanda could see people in it glancing out the window and talking, picking up cups of coffee and setting them down, completely unconcerned with the dark world outside.

Two trainmen jumped down and hauled the trunks and Margaret's suitcase onto a dolly, and rolled everything up to the baggage car. The conductor looked out the door of the nearest passenger car and shouted, "All aboard!"

"Goodbye!" Margaret said. She touched her mother's arm and then her father's and started walking fast for the train, without looking back.

The train engine was revving up loudly and so powerfully, and steam was spitting from places between the train's great black wheels. A train was nothing like a car, Amanda thought. It was thousands of times more powerful. Invincible, like time, which could never be stopped.

Amanda felt as if not just Margaret but the world itself were being ripped away from her, and she ran, catching up with Margaret, grabbing her sister's arm.

"Margaret, Margaret! Nothing will ever be the same!" she cried.

Margaret glanced at Amanda for just an instant and then jerked free. Amanda kept walking beside her all the way to the steps, hoping her sister would turn and look at her again.

"Margaret, Margaret, nothing will *ever* be the same!" she repeated, but maybe Margaret couldn't hear her over the sudden gathering roar of the train, because she didn't turn, she just ran up the steps of the train and disappeared inside it.

Amanda moved back and stood with her parents. In a minute they all could see Margaret again, standing by a window in the car just forward of where they stood, and then Margaret sat and looked out at them—her hands holding the seat in front of her around the little white napkin that covered the top of it, her face not smiling, as if she were looking out from another world.

The train started moving. Margaret waved once, whether to them or to all Rome, Wisconsin, Amanda didn't know. Then Margaret was out of sight, car after car following and the light from hundreds of identical square windows flashing by and erasing the place where Margaret's face had been, until the last car passed and the train was gone.

Just like that, it was over.

Their father sniffed a couple of times and took out his handkerchief. Their mother's gray-blue eyes were misty and excited.

To Amanda, without Margaret her family seemed tiny, standing on the crushed cinders by the rails, staring down the track where the train had departed.

"Well," said her father. They moved away from the depot toward the street. They heard bursts of singing when the door of the House of Truth Tavern opened and closed a few blocks away, but they couldn't make out the words. It was past eleven, and the street was empty, empty, except for one car coming, and then, even before it pulled up, Amanda could see whose it was. It was Roger Moss's old Ford and Roger was jumping out of it.

He didn't say hello, he just ran to the track with swift steps and stood looking down it, as they had done.

He raised a hand to shade his eyes from the streetlight so he could see into the distance better.

But there was nothing to see anymore.

Roger straightened and walked over to them. He was wearing his farm overalls and his face looked hard and tired and set. He looked up at the streetlamp beside the train platform, and the moths flickering around it, and even when he looked down and talked it was hard to tell if he was talking to her family or the moths.

"I decided to come. But I decided too late."

"When I write Margaret," Amanda's father said, "I'll tell her that you came."

"Thank you, Mr. Woods," Roger said.

Amanda felt a pang of jealousy. Her father was going to write to Margaret! He wrote lots of letters every day, but it was hard to think of his writing one that didn't begin, "Dear Mr. Smith, Your reservation for the 23rd is hereby confirmed." When she went to college, would he write to her?

Amanda's mother said, "Really, I'm surprised to see you here, Roger." She sounded very kindly but grand.

Roger's face hardened still more. His hands were in loose empty fists, and for the first time Amanda could figure how much heavy farm work he did, because he even had muscles on his fingers.

He looked at Amanda's mother.

"You know something, Mrs. Woods? It's a free country.

"Goodbye, Mr. Woods. Goodbye, Amanda," he said. And then he got in his car and drove away.

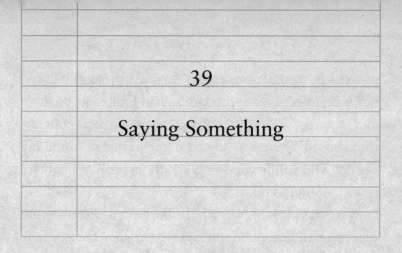

39

Saying Something

When Amanda was little, a storm had knocked down the biggest and tallest tree by their house, a tree that stood at the shore of the lake. Amanda had thought of the tree, a maple, as her special friend, and she had called it Old Brulie. Old Brulie had a very thick trunk and one very low branch that reached out over the water of Lost Lake. Amanda could climb up to that branch and put her arm around Old Brulie even when she was three years old. She still remembered the storm and how she had cried when a bolt of lightning hit the house and the wind came up and old Brulie fell.

Afterward, men had come to pull out the stump, but Old Brulie had been there so long and had such enormous roots that it took hours for them to hack all the pieces out. And when Old Brulie was gone, hauled away in a truck, the hole was so big Amanda thought it could never be filled. Her entire family had looked at the hole and nobody said anything, but Amanda had thought they should. There was something special you should say the day Old Brulie was gone, she thought. But whatever it was, nobody said it.

Margaret's leaving left a hole like that, a jagged empty place. Amanda wanted someone to say something, to say the right thing, but she didn't know herself what the right thing was; and, driving home, her parents didn't say a word.

They got to the house and her mother told Amanda it was time for bed. Her dad asked her mother if she wanted bourbon, scotch, or a martini. Amanda went in the bathroom and brushed her teeth.

She said good night to her parents and went into the bedroom and closed the door. She took off her fancy go-to-the-train clothes and put on her flannel pajamas with the little roses on them, but she didn't feel like staying in the room. She put on her slippers and padded softly out into the hall, staying out of sight, to listen to what her parents would say. One of them had to say something! Something important. Amanda felt that if they didn't, she would die.

She heard ice clinking in glasses, and she heard the snap of the cover of her father's cigarette lighter and the tiny sound it made when it whirred under his thumb to make a flame. No doubt he was lighting his pipe and probably her mother's cigarette. Amanda stood and waited.

"That Moss boy was extraordinarily rude," Amanda's mother said.

Amanda didn't really expect her father to say anything. When her mother complained about people, he usually didn't. He just let her go on talking.

"I don't think so," her father said, "I actually thought Roger was extraordinarily self-controlled." His voice sounded very cheerful, but tight and strained.

"That boy had no business coming to the station!" Amanda's mother said. "They had broken up. Margaret certainly didn't want him there."

Her father must have shifted his feet, because his chair squeaked. "I'm not so sure about that," he said.

"And Amanda!" her mother went on, just as if Amanda's father hadn't disagreed. "She means well, but she has a talent for saying the wrong thing at the wrong time. 'Nothing will ever be the same.' Margaret has her whole future before her. Naturally she didn't want to hear that."

"Amanda said what was on her mind," Amanda's father said. He sounded as if her saying what was on her mind was not a bad thing to do. As if it was maybe even a good thing. Amanda felt a tingle of gratitude and surprise.

Amanda's mother went on as if she hadn't heard him, like a train on the track of her own thoughts.

"Amanda's only interested in animals. Not people. That's what makes her awkward." Amanda's mother laughed gently. "She can't go more than a minute and a half without thinking about some bug or fish or horse or grizzly bear.

"Well, now that Margaret's gone, I'll have more time for Amanda. To shape her."

Amanda's father cleared his throat—a strangled sound. When he spoke, Amanda didn't recognize his voice. The voice sounded hot, like the voice of someone with a fever. She thought there must be another man in the room, but she knew there couldn't be.

"I wouldn't do that if I were you," Amanda's father said.

"Children need shaping. Amanda certainly needs it!" Amanda's mother said.

"Shaping people is one thing, Lydia, but if you go too far it gets beyond shaping. It gets into tearing them apart."

What did he mean, Amanda wondered. How could a person be torn apart?

"I'm sure I have no idea what you're talking about!" Amanda's mother said, using her offended voice.

"What you did to Margaret was a terrible thing."

Amanda felt her mouth open in shock, the air in the hallway dry on her tongue. Her father never criticized her mother! But now he was. Still her mother hadn't wanted to tear Margaret apart. She had just wanted to help Margaret. It had hurt a lot, but it had been help.

Amanda's mother's voice rose. "I didn't *do* anything to Margaret! She herself recognized that Roger Moss has no place in her future!"

"Maybe he doesn't. She's going into a big world. She's going to meet all kinds of people. Likely in a while they would have broken up themselves and had their own sorrow. But you didn't have to force them into it."

"I didn't force Margaret into anything! She herself decided it would be better if Roger didn't come to the station."

"Oh, did she?" Amanda's father said. His voice was low and hard and ugly. Amanda had never heard it like that. She wanted to say something, but she didn't dare make a sound. She rolled her fingers into fists, her fingernails cutting into her palms.

"Of *course* she didn't want that boy at the station! Margaret is brilliant. She's going places. I do believe she's going to be a doctor. How could I watch her go crazy about a farm boy and not go crazy myself?"

"Some people, Lydia, would say it was not your business."

"Some people would not have a daughter going to Wellesley, either."

"You spoiled something that will never be again. Roger is probably the first person Margaret has ever loved."

"Oh well, everybody has somebody—"

"Everybody doesn't. Some people never do. And I mean what I said. I mean he is the first person Margaret has ever loved."

Amanda remembered the night her father had talked to her about looking for someone you could make one world with. That was love. Her father believed in it.

"How silly!" Amanda's mother said.

She could make you believe anything was silly, Amanda thought, just with the tone of her voice.

"A boy with no future at all," her mother added.

"Everybody has a future, Lydia, and Roger's isn't a bad one. He is a very fine boy."

"A good-looking, fine farm boy." Amanda's mother could make being "fine" sound like being the worms at the bottom of the worm can. "I wish Margaret had had a boyfriend like Amanda's pen pal. He impressed me very much."

Her mother had liked Antoine! Now maybe her father wouldn't sound so angry. But his voice didn't change.

"If Antoine Bonnier lived next door instead of in

France, you wouldn't have been impressed," Amanda's father said. "With you, what's close is never good."

"That certainly is not true! Anyhow, boyfriends aren't Margaret's problem. She wouldn't have been so disturbed about leaving if it hadn't been for Amanda."

For her I can never act right! Amanda thought.

"Horse piss!" Amanda's father said.

"George!" Amanda's mother said.

"Amanda had nothing to do with Margaret's being upset—though she probably thinks she did, and if she doesn't think so, you'll convince her of it."

"I don't have to convince her. Amanda knows she's awkward," Amanda's mother said.

Amanda leaned against the hallway. Her Lyle Leveridge hand clutched her regular left hand, trying to protect her from what she heard. Her mother loved her but her mother looked down on her. Amanda wanted to cry.

"The world is an awkward place," her father said. "Being born is awkward. A lot of the time dying is awkward, too. And in between isn't mostly graceful. Amanda's no more awkward than you or me, or Margaret, or anybody else."

He was on her side! The way he saw things was the real way! Even Pam, who wasn't awkward, felt awkward sometimes. Maybe even Antoine, who was French, could feel that way.

"I know Amanda means well," Amanda's mother responded. "She's a good girl. As I said, all she needs is some shaping. Now that Margaret's gone, I'll have time for her. To give her the attention she needs."

"I have an offer to make to you, Lydia. You don't shape her. I will."

Amanda jerked upright, shocked.

"George, what do you mean?" Amanda's mother said.

"We have two children. You shaped Margaret the way you wanted to shape her and she made a lot of sacrifices to become the Margaret you wanted her to be. So now it's done. But if there's any shaping to be done on Amanda, I'll do it. You made the rules for Margaret; I'll make them for Amanda."

Amanda's dad wanted to be the one closest to her. Maybe he felt about her the way she felt about him—that they were of one blood.

"I never heard of such a thing!" Amanda's mother said.

"It's very simple. We have two daughters. We'll each raise one."

"People would think that is very strange." Amanda's mother's voice went up. "I know you don't care about what people think. You never *have* cared. But I do."

" 'People' don't have to know. Amanda doesn't even have to know."

"And you're going to take her to buy her clothes?"

"I will. Or she can pick them out herself."

"It would be a disaster. She'll wear fish lures on her blouses and birch bark in her hair. And it's your fault: you practically taught her to be a boy."

"So now," Amanda's father said, "I'll teach her to dance."

Amanda drew a deep breath. Her hands relaxed, then opened. For a minute she could feel them both, palms up, full of an unknown future.

Amanda could hear her parents getting up from their chairs.

"I want my daughters to be special!" Amanda's mother said. "I want them to do things I never had a chance to do. To be somebody. I hope you don't spoil that, George! I hope Amanda doesn't get hurt!"

If her dad didn't know how to raise her, Amanda wondered, would she get hurt? But her mother thought she knew how to raise Margaret, and Margaret had got hurt anyway.

"I can't say Amanda won't get hurt," her father said. "People suffer everywhere. But I do hope she will be her real self."

Amanda heard her parents move into the kitchen, set down their glasses. That meant they would be coming down the hall soon, going to bed. Amanda ducked into her room, straining to hear behind her nearly closed door. She heard her father say, "Our daughters are special. So are you, Lydia—if you would only realize it."

Amanda's mother didn't answer, but there was a sound of cloth rubbing cloth, the sound of a kiss. Were Amanda's parents hugging? They couldn't be. It was something they never did.

"I don't know," Amanda's mother said, sounding unlike herself, strangely young.

Her parents' footsteps passed in the hall. As they went by her door, Amanda's mother said something Amanda couldn't hear, and then, sounding like her regular self, "Just remember! You don't know a thing about raising a girl," and her father, laughing a strange painful laugh, said, "Well, maybe then I'll have beginner's luck!"

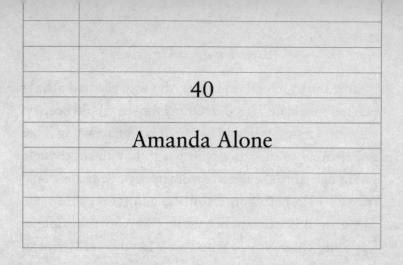

40

Amanda Alone

Amanda sat in the dark on the rug in the middle of the bedroom floor, thinking about her mother and her dad, and about being raised. She never knew they were raising her. She had thought she was just living.

She thought about her parents' fight. She felt sorry for her mother, for the way her mother had sounded.

But there were some good things to think of.

Her dad was going to teach her to dance. She remembered her dad's high-school yearbook, and the girl, Emily, who had written in it: "George, you are the best dancer!"

Dancing was not something the Lone Ranger ever did, not on one single show. But Amanda was getting beyond him.

With her dad making the decisions, maybe she could

wear jeans to school every day, the way she had always wanted to and no girls did. Or maybe she would keep on wearing dresses. It would be horribly embarrassing if her father came to the store with her to buy them, though. But in one store she knew a woman clerk who she would trust to help her choose clothes, and Pam could help. There would be other choices, too. Maybe next summer she could choose to go with Pam's family on their vacation, and experience the north country, the country without boundaries.

Her dad was going to make up the rules for her—but it sounded as if he wasn't even sure how to do it. At times, listening to his angry voice, she had been very scared, but she would keep doing what Pam had suggested: teaching him to talk to her. Maybe that way they could figure out the rules together.

She realized that she felt cold and her bottom hurt, and that she didn't need to be sitting on the floor in the dark. She wanted to see what the room looked like. The room, without Margaret.

She got up and turned on the light.

There wasn't much of Amanda's in it: her clothes in the closet, and some favorite rocks in a heap on the floor; on her bookshelf, her letters and her report card in the compartment of her diary.

The closet looked forlorn and the room looked very

bare. All Margaret's clothes were gone, and her jewelry, and her makeup. Margaret had taken all her clippings down from the bulletin board and untaped the pictures from *Mademoiselle* on the dressing table mirror. She had folded them all into her scrapbook, and taken them away.

In the wastebasket were scraps of paper the size of snowflakes that seemed to have been torn from Margaret's diary. Amanda didn't pick them up. She was glad she couldn't read them.

The only things on the bulletin board now were Amanda's Möbius strip; her photo of Antoine; a snapshot of Amanda from the third grade, in a Brownie troop that she had quit; and, in one corner, the fortune from Amanda's first fortune cookie, from the night at the new Chinese restaurant.

"You will be rich: wise laughter will be your golden treasure." Amanda hadn't thought of it in a long time, but she had put it up because she was sure it meant something important. Maybe someday she would understand it.

She opened the bed and slid between the sheets with their cold, damp feel of late August. She tilted her head and looked at the angels at the sides of the bed and the four-leaf clover in the middle of the top of the bedstead. The clover was quite dry, but it was still a real four-leaf clover. She was sorry Margaret hadn't taken it—and yet glad she still had it for herself.

She felt empty and strange. She missed Margaret, and yet she didn't.

You could not cut life up into good parts and bad parts. Life was like a Möbius strip, with two sides that were one. A person might want to separate the sides, but it couldn't be done.

Amanda snapped out the light, and, sighing, wiggled her feet.

Then she realized she was still lying inside her half of the bed, the way she always had. She didn't have to do that anymore.

She inched herself to the cold center of the mattress and stayed there till it felt warm. She lifted her right hand a little, and then her left. For a long time, ever since she and Lyle had changed hands, she had had the feeling that her right hand was a little heavier, a little stronger, than her left. But now her hands felt exactly the same.

Both had strength in them—the strength of Lyle's way, which was to know you were okay no matter what, and not to be scared of anything; and the strength of her own way, which sometimes seemed like wandering, but really was a kind of wondering—wondering forward into all the possibilities of life.

Amanda felt the power in her hands flow down into

her whole body. It wasn't magic power, of course. She knew that. Magic power was something you wished for but didn't ever get. The power was just human, the power of a person. But when you realized you had it, you could do first one thing, and then another and another, until there was no limit anyone could set to all that you could do.

Amanda loosened the blankets. She spread her arms and legs as far as they would reach.

She was growing. She could tell that from the bed. When she stretched, she nearly filled it.